CAST OF CHA

Richard Balron. A hard-working young lawyer with a temper, which leads him into a hasty marriage..

Mrs. Balron. His mother, whose bark is far worse than her bite.

Miss Ivy Balron. One of Richard's two maiden aunts, tart-tongued and fiercely argumentative.

Miss Violet Balron. Her sister, sweeter in temperament but no less stubborn. The two quarrel violently all the time.

Ada Terry. A gorgeous Broadway actress, known to Mrs. Balron as "the Red," who's related by marriage to the elderly sisters.

Doc Paunders. The town doctor, a friend of the Balron sisters.

Judge Mecklyn. Another of their friends, who gets together with them every fourth Monday.

Mr. Hernand. Another lawyer, also a friend of the sisters. Miss Violet considers all three of the elderly gentlemen to be her beaux.

Miss Dedingham. An elderly client of Richard's, who's also a regular at the Monday get-togethers.

Annie. The sisters' much put-upon maid.

Pat. Her husband, their gardener.

Oliver O'Brien. Nicknamed O.O., the town police chief.

Madge. She had always expected Richard would marry her.

Mrs. Evans. Richard's bossy secretary.

Plus assorted friends, clerks, cops, and townspeople.

Books by Constance & Gwenyth Little

The Grey Mist Murders (1938)*
Black-Headed Pins (1938)*
The Black Gloves (1939)*
Black Corridors (1940)*
The Black Paw (1941)*
The Black Shrouds (1941)*
The Black Thumb (1942)*
The Black Rustle (1943)*
The Black Honeymoon (1944)*
Great Black Kanba (1944)*
The Black Eye (1945)*
The Black Stocking (1946)*
The Black Goatee (1947)*
The Black Coat (1948)*
The Black Piano (1948)*
The Black Smith (1950)*
The Black House (1950)*
The Blackout (1951)*
The Black Dream (1952)*
The Black Iris (1953)*
The Black Curl (1953)

*reprinted by the Rue Morgue Press
as of March 2007

The Black Iris

By Constance & Gwenyth Little

Rue Morgue Press
Lyons / Boulder

About the Littles

Although all but one of their books had "black" in the title, the 21 mysteries of Constance (1899-1980) and Gwenyth (1903-1985) Little were far from somber affairs. The two Australian-born sisters from East Orange, New Jersey, were far more interested in coaxing chuckles than in inducing chills from their readers.

Indeed, after their first book, *The Grey Mist Murders*, appeared in 1938, Constance rebuked an interviewer for suggesting that their murders weren't realistic by saying, "Our murderers strangle. We have no sliced-up corpses in our books." However, as the books mounted, the Littles did go in for all sorts of gruesome murder methods—"horrible," was the way their own mother described them—which included the occasional sliced-up corpse.

But the murders were always off stage and tempered by comic scenes in which bodies and other objects, including swimming pools, were constantly disappearing and reappearing. The action took place in large old mansions, boarding houses, hospitals, hotels, or on trains or ocean liners, anywhere the Littles could gather together a large cast of eccentric characters, many of whom seemed to have escaped from a Kaufman play or a Capra movie. The typical Little heroine—each book was a stand-alone—often fell under suspicion herself and turned detective to keep the police from slapping the cuffs on. Whether she was a working woman or a spoiled little rich brat, she always spoke her mind, kept her rather sarcastic sense of humor, and got her man, both murderer and husband. But if marriage was in the offing, it was always on her terms and the vows were taken with more than a touch of cynicism. Love was grand, but it was even grander if the husband could either pitch in with the cooking and cleaning or was wealthy enough to hire household help.

The Littles wrote all their books in bed—"Chairs give one backaches," Gwenyth complained—with Constance providing detailed plot outlines while Gwenyth did the final drafts. Over the years that pattern changed somewhat, but Constance always insisted that Gwen "not mess up my clues." Those clues were everywhere, and the Littles made sure there were no loose ends. Seemingly irrelevant events were revealed to be of major significance in the final summation. The plots were often preposterous, a fact often recognized by both the Littles and their characters, all of whom seem to be winking at the reader, almost as if sharing a private joke. You just have to accept the fact that there are different natural laws in the wacky universe created by these sisters. There are no other mystery writers quite like them. At times, their books seem to be an odd collaboration between P.G. Wodehouse and Cornell Woolrich.

The Littles published their two final novels, *The Black Curl* and *The Black Iris*, in 1953, and if they missed writing after that, they were at least able to devote more time to their real passion—traveling. The two made at least three trips around the world at a time when that would have been a major undertaking. For more information on the Littles and their books, see the introductions by Tom & Enid Schantz to The Rue Morgue Press editions of *The Black Glove*s and *The Black Honeymoon.*

The Black Iris

1

Mrs. Balron placed a sizzling steak on the dining-room table, and admired it for a while before calling to her son.

"Richard! Dinner."

There was a rustle of newspaper as Richard Balron got up from his chair in the adjoining living room. He came through the archway and stretched a hand to switch on the light. "Spring is about on us, I guess."

Mrs. Balron yawned. "How clever of you to notice. But then, it so often comes after the winter."

Richard cut the steak expertly and said, "Drop it. I can't help it if I'm a bore."

"I saw Madge today."

"Hmm?"

"She's giving a party and wants you to come."

"Hmm."

"It's a week from Saturday night."

"Uh-huh."

"Look," said Mrs. Balron, "I'd have broken it more gently if I'd known it would excite you so. What are you going to wear? Maybe you're supposed to take a present—it might be her birthday. Actually, she didn't say what kind of a party, but maybe she'll tell you."

"Darned good steak," Richard murmured, and added, "Did she invite you?"

"Pointedly not. I'm to stay home and put up some preserves—or maybe go out to the ladies' sewing circle and kick up my heels."

Richard grinned at her. "I'll get you in."

Mrs. Balron sniffed. "Do you think I want to go to a party when I'm not invited?"

"Sure do."

"Well"—she picked a crumb from the tablecloth between her thumb and finger, and after regarding it absently for a moment, slipped it into her mouth—"how can you get me in?"

"I'll say I have no one to take care of you during my absence, so I'll have to bring you along."

Mrs. Balron snared another crumb, and said aggrievedly, "Ever since you grew up you've been making out that I'm one of these possessive, clinging mothers, just to further your own ends, mind you. I swear I think I'll move out of town. Why don't you get married and have a home of your own, you old maid, you."

"Any dessert?" Richard asked amiably.

"It's right there in front of your nose. I found a can of peaches that's been hidden behind the flour for months. And hurry up, will you? I want to go to the movies."

"Take off," Richard said, eying the peaches dubiously. "You don't have to help me with the dishes tonight."

Mrs. Balron stood up. "I'll just put the food away. I never can find it again if I leave it to you, not until it smells, anyway."

"Just once," said Richard, "and only once, I put the meat in the closet and the coffee in the refrigerator, so I have to hear about it for the rest of my life."

Mrs. Balron banged things in the kitchen for a few moments, and then returned to the dining room, dusting her hands. "Hey! I forgot! I saw the redhead in town today."

Richard abandoned the peaches, and his voice became alert. "I didn't know she was coming."

"Neither did I, but how would I know, anyway, unless you told me. And you couldn't tell me this time because you didn't know yourself, huh?"

"Pause a moment," said Richard, "and get the knots out of your tongue."

Mrs. Balron was smoothing her hair in the mirror over the sideboard. She glanced at her son and muttered, "It's downright mortifying. *My* boy must make a choice between a red-haired hussy and a nice girl like Madge."

Richard was piling dishes on the disordered table, and he said mildly, "It's not quite as bad as that. I could take a trip somewhere and maybe pick up something, or perhaps someone new will move into town."

Mrs. Balron buttoned up her coat, and sighed vastly. "I *do* wish I knew whether those two old bats are going to leave the Red anything or not. You should try and find out. And if they are, she'd be the better choice."

"Sure," Richard called from the kitchen. "Half isn't enough for me. I must have it all."

"Why not? Why should the money go out of the family? The Red is only a connection by marriage, while you're the only blood relative they have."

"Get going, will you? I'll run into town tonight and propose to Red—be safer all around. Only, what'll I do if she refuses me?"

"Refuses you!" Mrs. Balron snorted. "A handsome man with a hero's medal *and* a yellow convertible? How silly can you get?"

She made for the front door, and Richard called after her, "How can Red know I have a yellow convertible when you're using it all the time?"

He heard her back out of the driveway and roar down the street, and he grinned to himself. He'd better hurry with these dishes, though. He had some work to do at the office tonight.

Later, he walked through brisk, cold darkness to the town and enjoyed the clear night. His law offices were on the second floor of an old building on the main street, and he let himself in with his key, his mind on the young person who was known as "the Red" to his mother. Her name was Ada Terry, and he reflected that if he finished his work in time he might give her a ring, have a drink with her, or something.

He phoned her when he had disposed of his work without looking at his watch and thought that her answering voice sounded a little thick and stupid.

She said, "My God! Are you drunk, or something? Do you know what time it is? You woke me out of a sound sleep."

Belatedly, Richard glanced at his watch and discovered that it was eleven-thirty. "What are you talking about?" he demanded. "In your business it's barely twilight."

"I'm on vacation when I come to this town, so I go to bed at what you natives call a decent hour."

"Put on some lipstick and a scarf, or something, and meet me in the lobby. The coffee shop is still open, and I'm hungry."

"Why don't you go home and get a snack?"

"I'd have to get it myself, and eat alone. My mother does her washing at this hour. Come on, Ada. I'll be there in about ten minutes."

As it happened, he ran into Doc Paunders on the way, so it took him a little longer. Doc Paunders was middle-aged, but he had a nice shock of white hair that swept back from his forehead in waves, and he was tall and slim. He said to Richard, "You're in the doghouse for a fact. You were supposed to be there."

"Where?"

"You know where. This is the third Monday of the month."

"Oh." Richard looked down at his shoes and heaved a sigh. "Why don't you give me a ring when the day rolls around? You know I always forget."

"Of course, if you say so. But you should remember it without a nudge from me. Some day you'll be old too, and you'll find yourself sitting around waiting for people to come and see you. The rest of us always remember."

Richard continued to regard his shoes, and tried to look ashamed.

"Miss Ivy, in particular, was looking for you," Doc Paunders went on accusingly, and added with no inflection, "Miss Terry was there."

Richard looked up and said, "Oh?"

"Yes. At least *she* knows on which side her bread is buttered."

"Nuts," Richard said politely. "She isn't in town often, and it's natural that she should visit them when she does come."

"Very natural." Doc Paunders rocked gracefully from his toes to his heels. "What reason has she for coming to town except to put in a good word for herself? You'd better watch out. Miss Violet is very fond of the girl."

"So she's a nice girl, and she comes here for the express purpose of visiting them. They were good to her when she was a child. She owes them a lot, and it's decent of her to make a point of seeing them regularly."

"Decent and wise," said Doc Paunders, who hadn't bothered listening to all of it. "She's getting herself well thought of there, and if you don't look sharp you'll be done out of your rightful inheritance."

"Frightening. I'd have to live the way I'm living now—support myself for the rest of my life, like other men."

Doc Paunders gave him a lazy eye. "That's a nice, brave front, but you should have been there this evening."

Richard extended his wrist into the glow of a street light and said hastily, "I'm late for an appointment, Doc. I'll drop in there tomorrow, word of honor."

He hurried away, closing his ears to Doc's hurt murmur that he was merely speaking for the fella's own good.

Ada stepped out of the elevator as Richard entered the lobby of the hotel, and he hailed her with an easy smile.

"Fooled you this time, didn't I? I loitered, so that for once I wouldn't have to cool my heels waiting for you."

She gazed at him from the nimbus of her red-gold hair, and sighed, "I don't honestly know why I bother with you small-town hicks."

"Hicks? Plural? I'm not the only one?"

"You are the only one. My other beaux are city slickers of the most sophisticated type."

"That's all right, then. Come on, we'll have coffee or hayseeds, or something."

They went to the coffee shop, and after Richard had given an order he folded his hands on the table and said, "Well, how are the aunts? It seems that I should have turned up this evening, but I forgot about it."

"You're a louse," Ada said companionably. "Aunt Violet enjoyed herself, but Aunt Ivy was put out because you didn't come. Doc Paunders held forth on what's wrong with the world today, aided and abetted by Judge Meeklyn, and Miss Dedingham passed the remark that everything is preordained so that there's no sense in worrying, because it's going to happen, anyway. Mr. Hernand mostly kept his mouth shut, which was usual, and everyone enjoyed the sherry and cookies."

"It seems that I always miss the really good parties."

"There was one thing," Ada said thoughtfully. "When Mr. Hernand did get around to opening his mouth he asked the aunts why they kept their house lights on all night. They were decidedly fussed—you couldn't miss it—and Miss Violet said, 'We didn't think anyone would be passing at that time.' "

"At what time?"

"How should I know? Anyway, Miss Ivy said something about, 'Just *one* night, Mr. Hernand. I came downstairs for my medicine.' But I think she picked that out of the air. I wonder what they're up to?"

Richard shrugged and dismissed it, and proceeded to steer her to more entertaining subjects.

It was after two when at last he started for home, and he realized a little ruefully that the town's taxi and bus services were over and done with for the night. He'd have to walk it. He turned up the collar of his coat, and found himself thinking idly of Ada's story about Mr. Hernand. Well, he'd make a detour. He was so late now that it didn't matter anyway. See whether the aunts had all their lights on tonight.

There were not many houses on the street where they lived in their little white gingerbread sort of place. There was a lamppost directly in front of it, and as he approached he saw, with a little shock of surprise, that the house was lighted from top to bottom. He stopped under the lamppost and his eyes fastened on the front windows where the shades had not been drawn.

Miss Ivy and Miss Violet were clearly visible in the living room. They were fully dressed, and they stood at opposite ends of the room—and each held a revolver which was pointed at the other.

2

Richard ran up the front walk, stumbled on the two shallow steps that led to the veranda, and fell against the door. He twisted the handle frantically, found it locked, and moved over to the window. As he banged urgently on the glass he saw that Miss Ivy was now bending over a small chest of drawers in the corner, while Miss Violet stood in the center of the room with her hands pressed to her forehead.

Richard rapped again, sharply, and called out, "Aunt Violet! Let me in! It's Richard."

Miss Ivy straightened up and said something to Miss Violet which was accompanied by a peremptory gesture, and Miss Violet dropped her hands, nodded, and moved out of sight into the hall. Richard returned to the front door and stepped inside as his aunt swung it open.

She said faintly, "Richard, what is it? It's so late—"

He shut the door behind him and marched her grimly into the living room by the arm. Miss Ivy had her brows elevated and her eyes were chilly, but he did not wait for her to speak. He demanded, "Just what is this, anyway?"

She adjusted the black velvet ribbon that circled her throat, and observed, "That's about the way I'd have expressed it. We don't usually receive even relatives at this hour."

"Don't quibble," Richard said coldly. "You two were facing each other with guns, and you appeared to be about ready to shoot. What is it, a game?"

Miss Violet murmured, "Yes—yes, that's it. Just a silly game."

Miss Ivy nodded. "I should think we might be permitted our elderly amusements without panting nephews breaking in and breathing fire."

"More infantile than elderly," Richard said crossly. "Why don't you pull the blinds when you feel playful? And I did not break in. I was admitted."

"Perforce." Miss Ivy moved away from the chest of drawers and touched the leaves of a philodendron that was crawling over the edge of the mantelpiece. "What are you doing in the neighborhood at this time of night, anyway?"

"Never mind about the hour. I want to know what you two are up to now. Another one of your wild schemes, I suppose, and I don't like it."

"Perhaps you would like some wine," Miss Ivy suggested. "And cookies. We had expected you, you know."

Richard was annoyed to find himself slightly on the defensive. He started to refuse the wine, changed his mind, and heard himself saying apologetically, "I had to work tonight, and lost track of the time. I meant to drop in, got mixed up—"

Miss Ivy nodded. "Of course. I was disappointed, but I under-stand. We shall get you some refreshment." She nodded to Miss Vio-let, and they went together to the kitchen.

Richard waited until they had disappeared and then went straight to the small painted chest in the corner and opened the bottom drawer. They were lying there on top of some folded linens, not even de-cently covered. Two pearl-handled revolvers. He examined them and found that there was one bullet in each gun, and he was still turning them over in his hands when his aunts returned.

Miss Violet gave a little gasp, but Miss Ivy composedly lowered her tray onto the tiny table that stood in the center of the room.

"These are the guns you had," Richard said sternly. "There's a bullet in each one. What did you think you were doing?"

Miss Violet had backed up against the wall, and she whispered, "It's nothing, nothing at all. We—we have a right—"

Miss Ivy went to the small chest for the wine decanter. "Suppose you devote yourself to the practice of law and put those things back where you found them."

"I'm taking them with me," Richard said, looking her in the eye.

Miss Violet cried, "No!" and Miss Ivy poured wine without spill-ing a drop.

"We can't stop you if you decide to pilfer them, of course, but we can easily replace them. We have so many, some here, some in the big house. Father had a collection of them."

Richard was conscious of a swimming sensation in the head. He paced the room once or twice, and then sat down to the wine and cookies.

Miss Ivy asked politely if it was chilly outside, and he said it was. He poured more wine, rumpled his hair, and said, "Look, have you two had another argument?"

Miss Violet was now perched on the edge of a straight chair, and she spoke up like a spirited little canary. "We've always had argu-ments and we always shall. Why should it matter to you?"

"It doesn't concern me if you just argue, but when you get up and shoot at each other it's time someone stepped in and restrained you."

"We did not shoot at each other," Miss Ivy said impatiently. "I don't suppose it's criminal to point guns for fun. Your conversation is dull, and I'm bored."

Richard sighed and abandoned it. "How was the party tonight?"

"We had a lovely time," Miss Violet chirped. "Ada was here and everything."

"But you were not," Miss Ivy added.

"Well, no. But I've explained—"

"I heard you. But I want you to be here. It will make a big difference to you and to us."

"No, it won't," Miss Violet said cryptically.

Miss Ivy ignored her and glanced at the empty cookie plate. "Don't you have to get up in the morning?"

Richard nodded.

"Then you should be in bed."

"All right." He stood up. "I'm going. But look, please don't point those guns at each other again, will you? It's dangerous. In fact, I think I'll remove the bullets."

"You'll go home and get your sleep," Miss Ivy said firmly. "We'll take care of it."

They stood at the door together as he walked down the path, and he waved them a final good-by. After they had closed the door, he slid behind a tree and waited until the downstairs lights were turned off. When he saw a glow from the bedroom window on the second floor he left the tree and made for home with his shoulders hunched against the chill. Was it just a silly game as they had tried to make out? No, there was something more to it. He should have hammered it out of them.

When he reached home, he was forced to wend his way around the bathroom through a forest of damp, feminine underwear, and he wondered patiently why his mother must needs do her washing on Monday nights after the movies. She always claimed that it was the only time she felt in the mood.

He slept poorly through a series of fitful dreams, wherein his aunts stood facing each other with raised revolvers, and went down to breakfast the next morning with a headache. Several times, as his mother poured coffee and chattered of this and that, he opened his mouth to tell her about the aunts, and each time he closed it again. Better not say anything. She'd only spread it far and wide after swearing each of her intimate friends to secrecy.

"What's on your mind?" Mrs. Balron demanded suddenly. "You're not listening to me, which is usual, but you haven't even interrupted with one of your corny remarks about the weather."

He gave her an absent smile and murmured, "Just thinking."

"Then stop it. You'll damage the inside of your skull."

He went to his office and attended to the most pressing of his duties, but he left early for lunch. His secretary and woman of all work, Mrs. Evans, called after him that he had an appointment at three, and if he didn't show up he'd hear from her.

He went straight home at a brisk walk, but he did not go into the house. He circled cautiously to the garage, and saw with satisfaction that his car was there. He climbed in, started the engine, and backed out—and was not at all surprised to glimpse his mother making frantic signals from the front porch. He concentrated on his driving and pretended not to see her. It would only delay things if he stopped. She'd tell him she wanted to use the car and would arrange his transportation in some other fashion, send him out to Miss Dedingham's with the milkman or the laundryman. As a matter of fact, he wasn't speaking to the laundryman, who was being sued by one of his clients, and anyway, he didn't want his mother to know that he was going to see Miss Dedingham because she would certainly want to know why.

When he arrived he found Miss Dedingham standing in the sun in front of her barn, which had long been a garage, talking to her handyman. She was frankly elderly, with iron-gray hair and a heavy body that was jammed into a sweater and an old tweed suit. Her skirt advertised the age of the suit by stopping at her knees. Richard observed this obsolete style and reflected vaguely that somebody should have told her.

She turned at the sound of his car, and her rather forbidding expression relaxed a little. "Oh, Richard. You are the very person I wanted to see. I'm going to sue the Wrights."

Richard sighed because it seemed certain that a good deal of time would be wasted while he dissuaded her, but he said politely, "Tell me about it."

Miss Dedingham dismissed the handy man and led Richard to her house. It was a huge, shabby old place which had long since shed its elegance, and now sulked in the center of two acres of neglected lawn and shrubbery. Inside most of the place was shut off, and Miss

Dedingham lived and did her own work in a few rooms downstairs. Richard glanced up the wide, lovely old staircase and wondered how long it had been since anyone had mounted to the upper stories.

Miss Dedingham gave him coffee in the kitchen and explained at length how the Wrights' new dog spent all his free time in carefully destroying her vegetable garden. He knew that the vegetables formed a large part of her diet because her income was extremely small, and it took him some time to talk her out of a suit which he affirmed would be costly, and probably lost in the end. He added that rabbits were no doubt aiding the Wrights' dog in the destruction, and you couldn't sue rabbits. In the end he promised to bring some wire fencing and help her man, Joe, to erect it around the garden. She was inclined to refuse this until he explained that it was just some fencing he had left over, and the job would cost her nothing.

"Only," he said firmly, "I want some information from you by way of return."

She gave him a suspicious glance and sipped coffee with an air of having closed up.

"Are my aunts having any special kind of an argument?"

"They've always argued, and they'll go on as long as they've breath for it."

"I know, but I mean a special and particularly hot one?"

Miss Dedingham shrugged, and glanced down at her fingernails in faint embarrassment. They were dirty, so she hastily folded them into her palms.

"Well?"

"Oh, there's been a rather grim one going on for the past year."

"What's it about?"

"I couldn't tell you," she said quickly. "You really mustn't ask me things like that."

"Miss Dedingham"—he hesitated, and then went on earnestly— "I know I can talk to you because you're the only closemouthed woman in town. I saw the two of them last night at a late hour, through their front windows, and they seemed to be on the point of shooting each other with real guns."

Miss Dedingham exhibited no horror, nor any surprise. She merely said, "I shouldn't worry about them if I were you."

"But I *am* worried about them," Richard said peevishly. "How can I help it? You can at least tell me what you know. Do you expect me to find time to put up your fence if I have to use every spare minute running around trying to get them straightened out?"

Miss Dedingham eyed him speculatively. "Will you put a fence around the orchard too?"

To keep the kids out, Richard thought. That would be a big job, and expensive. Nor would she be able to pay for it.

He sighed. "All right. Tell me."

Miss Dedingham placed half a cigarette in her holder. While Richard supplied a light she made the usual explanation that she was trying to cut down for the sake of her health, and so smoked only a half at a time. It was well known that she couldn't afford as many cigarettes as she would have liked to smoke, and Richard said, "I'll throw in a carton of gaspers along with the fence."

She gave him a faint smile and murmured, "Don't be silly. As for Violet and Ivy, they are a pair of old fools. If they have nothing lying around handy to fight about, they scratch and dig until they bring something to the surface. I'll be frank about this, Richard, although I think it's all a great deal of nonsense. You must know that they make a new will on an average of once a year, but you probably don't know that they had to make separate ones last year because they could not agree on it. Miss Violet wants to leave the bulk to Ada, and Miss Ivy wants to leave everything to you, and they had to get Mr. Hernand to make two wills leaving the loot the way each wanted it until they've had time to fight it out to a finish."

Richard shrugged and gestured it away. "But the guns—why are they doing that?"

"Well"—Miss Dedingham reluctantly disposed of a butt that had begun to singe the end of her holder—"they think it's a good way, and perhaps the only way, to settle the argument. They are playing Russian roulette."

3

Richard could only stare at Miss Dedingham in speechless dismay, and she said mildly, "You know Russian roulette, don't you? There's just one bullet and you turn the cylinder and shoot. You have plenty of chances of living, and only one of dying. I believe you are supposed to point the gun at your own head, but they prefer it the way they're doing it, say it's more exciting."

Richard found his voice and exploded. "But, it's murder! Are they absolutely mad? They ought to be locked up somewhere!"

"You mustn't tell anyone," Miss Dedingham said uncomfortably. "I shouldn't have told you, of course." She added irritably, "Why on earth must they play their silly games in full view of anyone walking in front of the house? You see, if one of them does get killed, the other plans to say that it was an accident, that they were merely looking over their father's collection of guns. They ought to be more careful, though, even if their house is the last on the street, with no one opposite and no one likely to be walking out that way late at night. They pull this stunt once a month, after their Monday-night gathering, and Mr. Hernand *did* ask them why they had their lights burning so late. I suppose he could see the glow from his house down the street."

"They're insane!" Richard muttered. "They ought to be certified."

Miss Dedingham looked regretfully at her empty holder, and he automatically extended his cigarette case. She cut the new one in half with a knife and murmured, "I must not smoke more than a half at a time. So bad for me." She leaned back in her chair, puffing comfortably. "They've been at it every month for almost a year, now, and as a matter of fact, they did catch the bullet once or twice, but they're such rotten shots. I think Violet missed Ivy a couple of times, and Ivy said when she got her chance, she wouldn't miss, but she had *one* chance, and she *did* miss."

Richard jammed a fist across his forehead. "It's fantastic! What am I going to do?"

"Why don't you try minding your own business?" Miss Dedingham suggested. "It's their affair, and you've no right to interfere. They're old, and why shouldn't they die the way they want? Pity they can't shoot straight."

"I'm going down there now," Richard said grimly, "and do some straight shooting right into their four ears."

She laid a quick, restraining hand on his arm. "If you ever tell them I told you about this, I'll ruin you. And I can."

Richard grinned at her. "Threats."

She dropped her hand and sighed. "All right, I'll put it this way. Don't do anything to spoil the little pleasure they can find in this world, and mine. You see, I'd lose them as friends."

"Well"—he shrugged—"I won't do anything for a while. You say there won't be another shooting spree until next month?"

"Definitely not."

"I'll think it over, then, and keep my mouth shut in the meantime."

He went to the back door, and she called after him, "Don't do anything without letting me know, will you? I didn't think you'd take it so seriously."

He went down the back steps, and around the house to the driveway. " 'Seriously'!" he whispered. "Good God!"

He drove the car back to his mother's house, which looked both small and spruce in comparison with Miss Dedingham's decaying old mansion. He thought of the big house that belonged to his aunts, an even more elaborate affair than Miss Dedingham's. His father had been disinherited absolutely when he married, and the third girl, Mignon, had been treated in like manner when she married Ada's father. Grandfather, Richard reflected, had been a tough old nut who resented any migration from under his stern thumb.

Richard left the car in the driveway and hurried off. He did not know whether his mother was still at home, and had no intention of finding out. She'd have plenty to say to him, and he hadn't the time to waste.

At the office, Mrs. Evans asked if he had had lunch, and he shook his head. "Is there time? Wasn't there something?"

"At three," Mrs. Evans said firmly.

"All right. I'll be back in time."

He went to the Mayflower Shoppe. He would have preferred the hotel, but he was afraid of running into someone who would insist on lunching with him, and he wanted to think quietly by himself. At the Mayflower, he'd merely have to nod at the women, most of them friends of his mother.

He had overlooked the fact that his mother might be there, and she was. She did not want to join him, but from the midst of her four friends she called clearly, "That was a *nice* thing to do, running off in the car without so much as a word to me! I was very much put out, and Mabel had to pick me up, although her husband said if she ever got behind the wheel again, he'd divorce her."

Richard hid his face behind a menu, and from this haven ordered a cocktail. He tried to concentrate on his problem, but his mother's group was making too much noise; and then Ada came in and sat straight down at his table without pausing to blush or dally. Madge, Richard thought, would have waited to be asked, but Madge usually lunched at the hotel—more men there. This last thought flew in and out of his head in a hurry, and he felt that it was unworthy of him.

"Order me a cocktail, will you?" Ada said, squinting at herself in a small mirror.

Richard obeyed and was suddenly conscious of the fact that the noise of feminine chatter had died down considerably. He realized that he and Ada were being generally, if unobtrusively, observed, and he felt himself blushing slightly.

Ada put the mirror away and said directly, "What's the matter? You look hot, or embarrassed, or something."

"It's warm in here," he said stiffly. "Er, are you between plays just now?"

Ada blushed at this point and fiddled with the paper doily that lay in front of her. "Well, it's nice of you to put it that way. You could have said, 'Are you out of a job *again?*' "

"I didn't think of it. Are you?"

Ada sipped her cocktail and frowned at him over the top of the glass. "Not exactly. I mean, I have an engagement—should be good. It starts pretty soon, the rehearsals."

"Tell me about it."

"No, I won't," Ada said, not looking at him. "Might as well forget it while I'm here."

Richard wondered briefly why she didn't want to talk about it, and then shrugged it away. He hitched his chair closer to the table and said in a low voice, "Now listen. Our aunts are involved in some-thing really ugly, and it must be stopped."

"Tell me. I love gossip."

"I've had a plan jelling in my mind," he went on slowly, "ever since I heard about it from Miss Dedingham. But you're well mixed into the plan, and you may not like it."

"Plans are so often dull," Ada sighed. "Would you mind telling me what in the name of heaven you're talking about?"

"Still," Richard went on thoughtfully, "when you realize the danger in the situation you might agree. As a matter of fact, the aunts have been playing a form of Russian roulette."

Ada yelled, "What!" and everyone in the tearoom stopped eating.

Richard muttered, "Keep quiet, can't you?" and gave her the rest of it in a whisper. At the end he said, "I don't know whether this would interfere with your work, but if we tell the aunts we're going to get married, they'll have no reason to go on with their silly dramatics because the blasted money would go to both of us anyway."

Ada managed to get her mouth closed, and swallow, before she said feebly, "Sure, tell them anything you like, if it will stop them shooting holes in each other." She made further recovery during a moment of silence and asked in her normal voice, "Why doesn't each one leave her own money where she wants?"

"The whole load was left to them jointly with strict instructions from their father that the estate was not to be divided in any way. They never dreamed of going against his wishes, even after he died, and, as a matter of fact, that's the way they want to leave it themselves. One of us to get the big house, live there, and have all the money so that it can be maintained properly."

"Why don't they live in the big house themselves?"

"Oh"—Richard shrugged—"they say that they've always liked the cottage, and they're old, things like that. But their heir must live in style and carry on the old traditions."

"Aunt Violet," said Ada firmly, "must be balmy to want to leave it all to me. Not am I only a mere woman, but I'm not even a blood relative."

"It's the way she wants it."

Ada sat back in her chair and gave him a faint smile. "So you think we ought to walk around as an engaged couple for a few weeks in order to induce a ceasefire. What happens when we break the engagement? Do they shoulder arms again?"

"I hope to be able to think up something in the meantime, but this should take the pressure off for a while, anyway. We'll tell them that the engagement is to be kept an absolute secret, just among the four of us."

Ada laughed on a long breath and shook her vivid hair back from her face. "All right. You arrange it. But why don't you threaten them with the town cop?"

"They address the town cop as 'my good man,' and their pride is of solid steel. I'm only their nephew, and I'm only human."

"Richard," said a voice by his side, "pull up a chair for me. I see Miss Terry so seldom. I'll have my dessert here with you."

Richard swung a chair around from the table beside them and forbore to comment on his mother's rudeness in leaving four luncheon companions while she satisfied her curiosity, since it seemed probable that the companions had detailed her to this job.

He said loudly and clearly, "Ada has been telling me about her new play."

Ada gave him a blank look and proceeded to steer the conversation into domestic channels. She and Mrs. Balron were presently telling each other how they managed their housework and cooking.

"I have a small apartment in New York," Ada explained. "I love having a place of my own. Daddy was such a rolling stone, we always lived in boardinghouses and hotels."

"You are a home type of girl," Mrs. Balron decided. "You really should get married."

"Yes, but I like my work, too."

Mrs. Balron shook her head. "My dear, you can't have your cake and eat it. Children need a lot of attention."

"What children?"

"Your children."

"I haven't any," Ada said, her eyes wide and limpid.

"Well, of course. I mean, not yet, naturally. But—"

Richard stood up. "I really must go. I have an appointment."

They took no notice of him, and he stalked off, feeling vaguely offended. He glanced at himself in the Mayflower's full-length mirror, and then stopped for a better look. Talk about tall, dark and handsome! Ada and his mother took him entirely too much for granted. Maybe it was a lack of personality.

He was surprised to find his car standing at the curb. Hadn't his mother said something about Mabel having to pick her up? Just jabber, to make him feel properly ashamed. He glanced over his shoulder and put a tentative hand on the yellow door. Did he dare?

He climbed in and started the engine. This wouldn't take long, anyway. Just straight to his aunts' house and back again.

The aunts were not in, but their maid, Annie, led him to the living room and respectfully suggested cookies and sherry. He shook his head and glanced down at his watch. "I'll try them again. I haven't time to wait now."

Annie sighed. "You know, Mr. Richard, I ain't gonna be here much longer. I just simply can't take this place no more. I got the creeps all the time. The big house, now—I liked that."

"Aren't you used to that grave in the cellar yet?" Richard asked, smiling at her.

"Well—that one." She rolled a corner of her apron with nervous fingers. "But somebody is fixing a new one down there."

<h1 style="text-align:center">4</h1>

Richard had turned to leave, but he swung around again and stared. "What do you mean? Show me."

Annie shuffled her feet and looked down at the carpet. "I ain't supposed to go down there, but what I want to know is why not? I liked the old man, and what's wrong with puttin' a few posies on his grave?"

"I thought they kept the door to the cellar locked," Richard said.

"Door to the graveyard, you mean." Annie shook her head. "Them two sure must be nuts, livin' right over their father's bones. It was all right to hole him in down there. That's what he wanted, on account he was nuts too, but why do they have to come and squat on top of him?"

"Perhaps they wanted to be near him," Richard said with reserve. "How do you get down there?"

"Well, if you got to go," Annie said reluctantly, "I found a key."

"All right. Let's have it and open up. I want to go down and investigate."

"You can't go down now," Annie said, looking scared. "They'll come back and catch you."

"No, they won't, because you'll stand at the front door, and if you see them, you'll rush back and call down to me. I don't want them to know I've been snooping there."

Annie looked mutinous, but he handed her a five-dollar bill and she tucked it into her person somewhere. She extracted a key from a different spot, and he looked it over. It seemed to be an ordinary house key, interchangeable with a hundred others, and hardly worth the five spot, but he said nothing as he followed her to the kitchen. She unlocked the door that led to the cellar, and switched on the light for him.

"I won't be long," he told her, "but you go to the front door and watch. I don't want to be caught."

He went down the narrow stairs and stood for a while shaking his head at his grandfather's black marble tomb. Annie was right. The old buster must have been nuts. There'd been trouble getting permission for this, but here he was, cozily buried in the cellar of the cottage. Perhaps he'd ordered his daughters to come and live with his remains so that he wouldn't be lonely.

Richard shrugged and began to move around the small space. It was not like an ordinary cellar. The whole place had been painted a dark gray, and all the pipes were covered. There were no washtubs, and the furnace had been installed in a small room that was built on to the back of the kitchen. The high, narrow cellar windows had been paned in stained glass, and the floor was covered with linoleum of a very dark gray.

On his first tour Richard was unable to find that anything had been disturbed, but he searched a second time, more carefully, and found that the linoleum had been cut in a neat oblong over in one corner. He knelt down and pried at it with his fingers, and it came up quite easily. There was a piece of plywood underneath, and he pulled that up to find an excavation, one quite large enough, and of the right shape, to be a grave. It didn't have to be a grave, of course, Annie's fears to the contrary. He pulled at the linoleum around the edge, discovered that it had been laid on a dirt floor, and shook his head. Bad workmanship. It would never last. He remembered that his aunts had had the heating system installed when they moved in, and supposed that the old man had used this cottage as some sort of a summer house. Well. He stood up, dusting off his hands.

He went upstairs and called to Annie, who came back and locked the door again. She whispered, "You seen it?"

Richard nodded absently.

"I'm tellin' you I don't like it, and I ain't stayin'."

"You don't sleep here, do you?"

She shook her head. "There ain't no room for me. I stay over at the big house with Pat."

"Oh yes, Pat. How is he these days?"

"He aches here and he aches there," Annie said without interest. "Gives him something to talk about."

"How did you find that hole in the cellar?" Richard asked. "Were you looking for something?"

"Nope. Just snoopin'. I went over to look at one of them fancy-colored windows, and I tripped on the linoleum."

"I wonder who's been digging down there," Richard said thoughtfully. "It could hardly be my aunts. They're too old and frail."

"They're thin," Annie said with a faint scorn, "but they ain't so frail. Nor they ain't so old, neither. Late sixties. I got a grandmother pushin' ninety. Now look," she added with sudden decision, "you better leave me get you some cookies and stuff, or I'll get bawled out for not feedin' you."

Richard glanced at his watch and remembered vaguely that he had to be somewhere at three, but there was still a little time. He sat down in the living room and said, "O.K. Bring on the nourishment."

The Misses Balron came in just after Annie had supplied him, and they sat down to nibble cookies and sip sherry with him.

"We haven't had anything since breakfast," Miss Violet said, settling her skirt. "So this can be our lunch."

"Very interesting," Miss Ivy observed repressively.

Miss Violet selected a cookie with great care and added, "We took our walk."

"Have you anything special on your mind, Richard?" Miss Ivy asked.

"Well, yes, I have, as a matter of fact."

"As a matter of fact," said Miss Violet sunnily, "you never do come for just a visit."

"Why should he?" Miss Ivy demanded. "Your dull conversation would keep anyone away."

Richard murmured, "Please!" and shifted uncomfortably on his chair. "You know I've been here just to visit. But I don't like to drop around at any time. You have your own affairs and your own friends, and I might be a nuisance."

Miss Ivy nodded. "That is quite right, Richard, but you really should attend our Mondays."

"Oh, yes, yes, certainly. I shouldn't dream of missing them." He caught Miss Violet's eye and added hastily, "As you know, I was tied up with work at the office last night. Very pressing. Really couldn't leave it."

"We have no wish to interfere with your business," Miss Ivy agreed. "I am sure you would have come had it been possible."

Richard recrossed his legs and eased his collar with a nervous finger. "I, er, came today to give you some news I thought would interest you."

Miss Violet gave him an impish little smile and chirped, "Anything that concerns you, dear, is naturally of the greatest interest."

"All right, that will do," Miss Ivy interrupted coldly. She glanced at Richard and asked, "What is it?"

He drank sherry and set the glass down carefully. "Well, as a matter of fact, I'm engaged. I mean, we are—Ada, you know—and I."

Miss Violet clapped her little hands and gave a trilling laugh. "Why, that's wonderful!"

Miss Ivy's straight back and square shoulders relaxed a little against her chair. "Well." She nodded. "Yes, I am pleased. But of course she'll have to give up the stage."

"Oh no!" Miss Violet's small face flushed pink. "She will not!"

"Indeed, she will!" Miss Ivy did not bother to look at her sister. "I understand that she is a good cook and a fair housekeeper. I think she is qualified to be your wife, Richard."

"His mother can cook for him, as she always has," Miss Violet cried angrily, "and then Ada can go away when she needs to and come back if she wants to—"

"Are you out of your mind?" Miss Ivy demanded. "In the first place, she must stay by her husband's side, naturally, and in the second place, his mother can't cook for him because he'll have to live in the big house, and *she* can't go there."

Richard took in breath, but Miss Violet was ahead of him. "Well, of course I know they must take their rightful place in the big house, with enough money to keep it up—"

"We shall assume the expenses." Miss Ivy's forefinger tapped the arm of her chair, and she looked directly at Richard. "You can use your income for your personal expenses. *But*, Ada will have to stay by your side as your wife and mistress of the house. I believe she can give you the background you should have, and I tell you frankly that I'm glad you didn't choose that common little Madge."

"Madge is not common," Richard said indignantly, "and my mother wouldn't dream—I mean, we don't need a big house—"

"Mother's wedding veil," Miss Violet prattled contentedly, "really lovely. But she must have a new dress. I often think that ice blue they sometimes wear, or blush pink, is pretty."

"Ivory satin of the best quality," said Miss Ivy, and added in an outraged whisper, "Ice blue and blush pink! Vulgar!"

Richard stood up. "I must go. I have an appointment. You won't tell anyone about this, will you? Ada wants it kept quiet for a while, and you are the only ones who know. We thought it would please you."

"Oh, why?" Miss Violet began, but Richard said hastily, "I have to run. Good-by. I'll see you."

He hurried out to his car and drove swiftly back to the Mayflower Shoppe. He looked inside, found the place empty, and resignedly drove the car to his house, where he parked it in the driveway.

He returned to his office on foot and found Mrs. Evans pleasurably excited over having bad news to impart. "You're just barely in time to make that appointment, and your car's been stolen."

"It's sitting in the driveway without a scratch on it."

"Oh." Mrs. Evans was disappointed. "Well, you're supposed to go to the police station and give them all the details."

"Don't tell me she reported it to the police!" he groaned.

"Of course. Why not?"

He went off to keep his appointment and decided to let the car business iron itself out. He was late getting home, and Mrs. Balron met him with a decidedly stony face.

"Sorry, Mother. I intended to get the car back to you within a few minutes, but something came up. Couldn't even phone you."

"Oh, don't mind me. I'm only your mother. It's your car, after all."

He hung his coat and hat in the hall closet and said mildly, "You're in a real tantrum, aren't you?"

"It's my own fault, and I'm willing to pay for the extra tickets we'll have to buy for the policemen's ball. I should have known you'd taken it. Come on, dinner's ready."

As they sat down at the table Richard said, "We'll get another car. You can have the yellow job. You picked it out, anyway."

"What would you use for money?"

"If I scrape the sides and bottom of the account, I think there'll be enough."

Mrs. Balron looked full at him and said in a peculiar voice, "Hadn't you better save what you have?"

He lowered a loaded fork and sat back in his chair. "High dudgeon? What *has* ruffled your feathers?"

"Have you seen the evening paper?" she asked ominously.

"No. What's in it?"

"Right on the front page," said Mrs. Balron furiously, "where you can't miss it. You couldn't tell your mother first, you had to take it to the newspaper. Here I am lunching with my girlfriends today and I can't tell them, *because I don't know*. What are they going to think of me?"

Richard pushed his chair back violently and made for the living room, where the evening paper was sprawled across the couch. He rustled the sheets feverishly until he found the first page—and there it was. Pictures, too. It stated that the lovely Broadway Stage Star, Miss Ada Terry, would marry Local Lawyer.

5

Richard made a series of sounds in which there were no recognizable words, and Mrs. Balron let out a cry.

"Now, *don't* lose your temper. There's nothing to get mad about. I don't care, anyway—"

Richard turned and stalked back to the dining room, and she hurried after him. He was in one of his dreadful tempers, and she simply didn't know how to cope with them. He sat down and began to eat at a furious rate, and she eyed him uneasily.

"I don't know why you don't keep your shirt on. I suppose you swore that girl to secrecy, and she broke her oath, to the newspaper, too. So what's the idea of keeping it secret, anyway? Evidently *she* doesn't mind who knows, and why should she?"

"Why, indeed?" Richard said through his teeth. "Big, handsome lawyer, like myself. Did you know that we are going to live in style in the big house, and that she will have to give up the stage?"

"Is that so?" Mrs. Balron murmured, and batted a piece of pie around the plate with her fork.

"About you—"

"Don't you worry about me," she said quickly. "Just leave me out of it. I have my own house and my own money."

"Yes. Well, I think that will be best. Of course, Miss Violet thought you ought to live with us so that you could cook my meals while Ada is off appearing on the stage, but Miss Ivy turned thumbs down. Said you could not live in the house, and Ada would have to stay by my side and attend to my needs."

"Those two old bats," said Mrs. Balron clearly, "can mind their own business, if they have any, which they don't. And that's what's the matter with them. I guess I can live where I please without running to ask them. And of course you could tell them this tremendous secret, but you had to keep it from me."

Richard stood up. "I haven't time for the dishes tonight. You can leave them on the table until I get back. I have some business to attend to."

"Oh, yes, to be sure." She followed him out to the hall. "But let me tell you something. You're going out in a temper to do something you'll be sorry for, and I will *not* cover up for you this time the way I have in the past. If you had any sense, you'd go straight up to bed where you'd be safe, and keep out of trouble."

He combed his hair at the mirror and put on his hat.

"You look silly with a hat on, you know it?" Mrs. Balron observed.

"Naturally. Since I feel silly, and am silly. Good night, madam."

He walked across the lawn to where his car was parked in the driveway, and she yelled after him, "Where's your coat? It's cold tonight."

He heard her and realized that it *was* cold, but he got into the car without replying. He wouldn't go back for his coat now. Let it rot on its hanger. He stretched an arm to adjust the little mirror over the wheel, and saw that his hat sat firmly and quite straight upon his head. Well, that was the way he felt. The mirror was loose, too, what with the two of them changing it to suit themselves every time they got into the car, and it could stay loose and fall off its hinges.

He backed into the street and headed for town. See what Ada had to say. Not that he didn't know perfectly well. She must have stumbled over her feet rushing to the newspaper in order to make the evening edition. Not that that mattered so much. It would probably have got out, anyway, but the thing was that she *could* keep a secret if she wanted to, and keep it well. She was simply using him. And why couldn't she have explained everything when she had the opportunity? She wanted the engagement announced in the newspaper for reasons of her own, and why not say so? Of course, he might have refused that—his own private affairs. But she didn't care—make things right for herself, and that was all that mattered.

He parked in front of the hotel in a space that would have been too small had he not simply headed into it and run one wheel up on the sidewalk. He left it that way and pushed through the door of the hotel in such a hurry that he collided with a woman ahead of him, and very nearly knocked her down. He righted her and apologized, received only a glassy stare, and followed her as she made her way to the desk.

He waited glumly until Clarence Hill, the night clerk, had disposed of her, and then he said abruptly, "Give Miss Terry a ring and tell her I'm here and want to see her."

Clarence nodded and reached for the phone. He gave an undertaker's restrained smile and murmured, "May I offer my congratulations?"

Richard glared, and Clarence hastily gave his entire attention to the phone. After a moment he said, "Go right up."

Richard went right up. He felt that the elevator was too slow for his mood, so he ran up the stairs that encircled it. He saw it trundle slowly down, and then up again, and was further infuriated when it reached the third floor before he did.

He walked down the hall and knocked loudly on Ada's door, and when she opened it he brushed past her into the room with his hat still on his head.

Ada looked him up and down. "This is my room, you know. You'd better go out again and wait until I ask you in."

He retreated to the hall and stood looking at her.

"If you remove your hat, you may come in."

He stalked in and waited until she had closed the door and seated herself, and stonily ignored an invitation to have a chair himself.

She smiled up at him carelessly. "Well, shouldn't you start the small talk? You came to see *me*."

Now that he was facing her he couldn't seem to think of the right things to say. He wanted to dispose of some withering sarcasm, but the words would not assort themselves. In the end he muttered, "I need a couple of drinks before I can get this off my chest."

"Good." Ada stood up. "I wouldn't mind a drink. I'll go with you."

They descended to the lobby in silence and went to the bar in the rear. As they walked in Doc Paunders, Judge Meeklyn and Mr. Hernand rose from a table at which they had been sitting together and gave three polite little bows. They shook hands with Richard, offered congratulations, and insisted that there must be drinks all around by way of celebration. They pulled up two more chairs, and Judge Meeklyn ordered while Doc Paunders said genially, "We are all very pleased with this engagement."

Mr. Hernand coughed. "It's, er, very sudden, is it not? Have you thought it over carefully? Young people are apt to be so impulsive."

"Now, Hernand," Judge Meeklyn said repressively, "this is a festive occasion. Let the young enjoy life as they find it. People who are always thinking of tomorrow miss a lot of fun."

"Whatever happened to Madge?" Doc asked. "We always thought—well, you know."

Richard frowned. Yes, they'd always thought, and he *did* know. He'd been thrown at Madge's head for as far back as he could remember. People trying to lay out his life for him—and he'd thought of marrying Madge, often. But he was through with all that. He'd marry anyone he pleased, and where and when he pleased, too. As for Ada, she'd be the sort of wife who'd be off attending to her career most of the time, and carrying on with the men in the cast.

Well, he knew what they could do as far as he was concerned, all of them. His hand tightened around his glass, and he drank a silent toast to himself.

Judge Meeklyn was saying, "As soon as I saw the paper tonight I phoned your aunts and asked them when the wedding was to be, but they didn't know."

Doc Paunders stretched his legs and puffed, "I don't suppose the happy groom-to-be knows either."

Richard glanced at Ada. Smiling, not with him, but at him. He had to wipe the smile off her face.

"Oh, yes, I know. It's tomorrow."

6

There was a dead silence, and the smile faded from Ada's face. Her eyes became hard, and she was the first to speak.

"Yes, it's to be tomorrow."

The three men expressed surprise, and Mr. Hernand was heard to murmur that it seemed a little soon. Doc Paunders took in breath to express an opinion, but was drowned out by the voice of Mrs. Balron.

"Oh, there you are, Richard. I've been looking high and low for you."

"Why?" Richard asked coldly.

She slid into a seat at their table and said with elaborate carelessness, "Well, I just, er, thought I'd find out what you were doing."

Judge Meeklyn cleared his throat ponderously. "It is, perhaps, just as well that Richard is getting married so promptly. A son living with his mother, you know—the mother is usually inclined to become too possessive."

"Is that so?" Mrs. Balron summoned a waiter and ordered a drink for herself. "Then maybe you can tell me how to get him married off."

Mr. Hernand looked puzzled. "But surely you know that he is being married tomorrow?"

Mrs. Balron was startled, but she hung on to her poise. "I knew I'd catch up on the gossip when I joined this group. Er, who's the bride?"

Ada stirred. "I am."

"You're not blushing or giggling, or anything."

"I am nervous, naturally," Ada said stonily.

"I see. Would you care to come upstairs to your room with me for a few minutes? I'd like to speak to you."

Ada started to refuse, but Doc Paunders stood up and pulled her to her feet. "You go along, young one. You shouldn't be seeing him tonight, anyway. His mother ought to be able to give you some valuable pointers on how to handle a husband."

Mrs. Balron laughed briefly. "Sure, I'll tell her. It's the same with any man, and it's very simple. Get the better of him before he gets the better of you. Come on, Ada."

They went off, and Doc Paunders sat down again. "Now that the women have gone, we can give Richard a bachelor's celebration."

"He's gone too," Judge Meeklyn said, indicating Richard's empty chair. "He just slid out after them."

Mr. Hernand shook his head. "There is something very odd about this entire affair."

Doc Paunders leaned over the table. "It's worse than odd—why, they hardly know each other. My guess is that she's giving him money to marry her. You know these actresses. They get into trouble of all kinds, and sometimes they *have* to have a husband."

Mr. Hernand blushed. "Do you think she is, er, *enceinte?*"

"Ah, no, not that. These stars are gay birds, and sometimes the women fight among themselves. She might be going around with some other dame's husband, so she pays for a husband of her own who will keep quiet."

Judge Meeklyn frowned and folded his hands in front of him. "Richard is doing well, financially, and I don't believe he is the type who would accept money from a woman for such a purpose."

"No," Mr. Hernand agreed. "He would never lower himself in that way."

"Ah, there are plenty of men who'll do anything for money," Doc Paunders snorted. "Anyway, maybe he wants to marry her. He might be in love with her."

"But what about Madge?" Mr. Hernand asked.

Judge Meeklyn shook his head. "He's not in love with Madge. He could have married *her* ages ago."

"I don't agree," Mr. Hernand said primly. "Nor do I believe that Richard would give that girl his name just for money."

"Your ideas smell of mothballs," Doc observed. "But then, they always did."

Mr. Hernand's face stiffened, and Judge Meeklyn said, "You are both being absurd. Those two children love each other."

"Sentimental Joe," Doc yawned.

Mr. Hernand got to his feet. "I am going home. I can see no reason for sitting here and bickering with you two." He gave them a chilly nod and made off.

"I'm going too." Judge Meeklyn pushed his chair back. "Now don't spread those wild ideas around, Doc."

"Oh, go and boil your head. I consider it my duty to knock on every door in the hotel and dish the dirt."

Judge Meeklyn frowned and departed, and Doc ordered another drink.

In Ada's room Mrs. Balron had no sooner settled herself comfortably than Richard walked in. She gave him a cold eye and said, "You wait downstairs."

"While you fix things? Nothing doing."

"I'm sure I don't know what you think you're doing up here," Ada said.

"I've come to discuss arrangements for the wedding."

"Oh?"

"Yes."

"Well, go ahead."

Richard picked up the phone and put through a call to his aunts, and while he waited for the connection he felt some of the heat of his anger drain away into a mild glow. He began to regret his impulse and glanced uneasily at the two women. They were watching him expectantly, and he cleared his throat and spoke.

It took some time, but when at last he cradled the phone everything had been settled. Miss Ivy would arrange it, organist, minister, cake, wine, and guests. She was somewhat put out when he told her to expect his mother, since she obviously regarded her as an intruder, but she reluctantly agreed to make the best of it.

There was an expression of astonishment, and even shock, on Ada's face, and Mrs. Balron said shrewdly, "This is a sudden marriage, isn't it?"

Richard gave her a cold smile. "Quite sudden, yes. Well, good night, darling. Don't forget that we must go around and get a license in the morning. I'll make it late for you. Eleven o'clock all right?"

He kissed Ada's rigid lips and bowed himself out. That would put a scare into her, teach her to think a bit. They could get the license in the morning, all right, but she probably didn't know that they'd have to wait three days before they could use it. Maybe he could get something arranged by that time, think up a way to stop those two infernal women from shooting at each other. Maybe he could persuade them to live apart. Put Miss Violet, perhaps, in with Miss Dedingham. Miss Dedingham would have to open up another room, but she could use the money. Shame for that nice old place to be used as a sort of camp. But the aunts' big house was in excellent condition. It would be a nice place to live, even with Ada, the celebrated Broadway star. He laughed grimly to himself. She'd know how to handle it, all right— the best arrangement for the furniture and ornaments, the right clothes for herself. She'd move around there with real elegance. Madge, well, Madge would be better in a cottage with a frilly apron, cooking delicious food until they both got too fat.

He stepped out of the elevator into the lobby and came face to face with Madge herself.

She said, "Richard!" and her posture and expression changed for the better. "Why, I haven't seen you forever."

"Hello, Madge." He grinned at her. "I've been busy. Where are you headed at this time of the night?"

"Oh, I came into town with Mother, shopping, and then we had a bite to eat, and I dropped her at the movies. I'd seen the picture, so I thought I'd look in on Ada. I heard she was in town. I want to invite her to my party."

Richard took her arm. "Don't go up now. She has a guest. Come and have a drink with me."

"Why, I'd love to," Madge said with one hand patting uneasily at her hair.

She asked for rye and ginger ale, and Richard ordered a scotch and soda for himself. She had pulled a small mirror from her purse, since she was unable to stand the strain of speculation on her appearance, and she was making darting little rearrangements of the curls at the side of her face. "I'm so glad I ran into you, Richard. I never did hear whether you were coming to my party. I spoke to your mother about it, you know."

"Yes, certainly. Wouldn't miss it for anything," Richard said amiably. "Is your mother going to be there?"

"Well, yes. I mean, Mother lives with me, after all."

Richard laughed gaily and ordered another scotch. He felt almost lighthearted. "You might as well invite my mother too. She can talk to yours about their elderly affairs, leaving us free to cut capers."

Madge flushed and looked down at her drink, and Richard rubbed his hands. "Good. That's settled, then. I'll tell her. I know she'll accept, she loves a party."

Madge compressed her lips, but she said nothing. That Mrs. Balron was a *pest*, and she didn't want her horsing around and spoiling things. She never sat and talked quietly with people of her own age at a party. Instead, she circulated among the young men, and of course they always had to be polite and give her a lot of attention. And then Ada had to be asked as well. She *would* have to come to town just at this time. Oh, the party was ruined, unless Ada was leaving soon, and Mrs. Balron got sick.

She leaned toward Richard and began to speak animatedly of other things, and their heads were close together when Ada and Mrs. Balron walked into the bar.

Mrs. Balron saw them at once, and she stopped and put a hand on Ada's arm in a dramatic gesture. "My dear, look! Your bridegroom flirting with another woman. Already. Really, Ada, I wouldn't put up with it. Walks into a bar and picks up a woman—"

"Hush," Ada said with a smothered giggle. "People will hear you."

Richard looked up and saw them, and got to his feet immediately. "Well, well. Mother and Ada. We'll move to a larger table, Madge, so that we can all be together."

He herded them into a group and ordered drinks, including another scotch for himself. Madge was still making uphill work with her first rye and shook her head a little coldly.

"Well!" Mrs. Balron settled herself and accepted her drink cheerfully. "Suppose we drink a toast to the wedding."

Madge raised her head and asked in a scared voice, "What wedding?"

No one answered or even heard her. Miss Ivy and Miss Violet had appeared at the door, and after a moment's hesitation crossed the room to stand in front of Richard.

"You must come at once," Miss Ivy whispered. "There is a dead man in our living room."

7

"What do you mean!" Richard demanded. "Are you serious? Who is it?"

"We don't know," Miss Violet whispered. "We—we didn't look."

"We had just come in," Miss Ivy explained. "We were frightened, naturally, and we ran out again and got back into the car. We telephoned your house, but got no answer, so we came here."

Richard bid an abrupt and hasty good night to the three women at his table and urged his aunts out into the lobby. "You drive back to your house, and I'll stop and pick up the chief. We'll be out there before you."

"No." Miss Ivy planted her sensible Oxfords directly in front of him. "We are both too nervous to handle the car. You'll have to drive back. And I will not have the chief unless it is absolutely necessary. I want *you* to investigate first. The man may not be dead, just a seizure, perhaps. e was lying on his face."

"Well"—Richard decided not to waste time in argument—"we'll pick up Doc Paunders, then. Come on, get in. I'll drive you."

They got in, and Richard, in the driver's seat, suddenly felt rather helpless. The car was an old electric, and the aunts had always declared that it was much easier to drive than what they called "these modern saloons." There was a rod instead of a steering wheel, and the interior, decorated with a bunch of artificial roses, had the air of a cozy parlor. Miss Ivy seemed to be facing him, and Miss Violet was off to his side somewhere.

"Listen," he said desperately, "can't we go in my car for once? It will be much quicker."

They refused indignantly. Modern cars were dangerous, and in any case, their own might be stolen if it were left in town all night and they would have great difficulty in getting another.

Richard gingerly set the antique in motion and shook his head. "What makes you think anyone could steal this, when it would take him an hour merely to get out of town? If that man wasn't dead when you saw him, he'll never last until we get this crate out there."

"Oh, I'm sure he was dead." Miss Violet shivered. "He was so still, you know."

"This car is not a crate," Miss Ivy said austerely.

Richard had a vague feeling that if he could help along by putting his feet through the floor onto the road beneath, they'd make better time. He tried to hang onto the rod, and to keep his hands from feeling uneasily for a wheel, and was almost surprised when they drew up in front of Doc Paunders's house. The doctor was reading in his study, but he agreed to come, and seemed pleased at the diversion. Richard would have preferred another medical man, who was generally known as "the young doctor," but he realized the futility of any such suggestion. The young doctor was out of favor with his aunts, since he had had the presumption to recommend an operation for Miss Violet. It had been merely a matter of removing her tonsils, but still, an operation, in the hospital and everything.

Doc Paunders joined them in the wheeled parlor, and Richard headed for the aunts' house, with Miss Ivy giving him instructions in driving all the way. Doc Paunders kept muttering, "Now who could it be?" until they approached the house at last, when he changed his tune to ask "Why don't you lock your doors when you go out, anyway?"

"We always lock our doors," Miss Ivy said furiously. "It's that feckless creature, Annie. I expect she left the back door open. We had to go before she left. So many things to arrange, and so little time."

Doc Paunders lighted a cigar and dropped the match into the vase that held the artificial roses. "You two shouldn't be wandering around alone after dark."

"We were not 'wandering,' " Miss Ivy snapped. "And I'll thank you to fish that match out of there. We don't allow smoking in this car."

Richard halted the ancient vehicle and got out with a sigh of relief. He saw that the house was lighted and the front door standing open, and he left Doc Paunders to attend to his aunts while he hurried up the path. Lights were on in the hall and the parlor, and he looked around quickly, but there was no sign of any man, either prone or upright. He pushed at the heavy drapes that closed off the dining room and was fumbling for a light in there when he heard Miss Violet say, "We were so frightened that I guess we just ran out and forgot to close the door." There was a moment of silence, and then she let out a little cry. "He's gone!"

Richard turned back and found both his aunts staring down at the neatly carpeted floor. Doc Paunders thumped his black bag down onto a table and asked crossly, "What's the matter with you two, anyway?" He looked distinctly disappointed.

Miss Ivy glared at him. "I tell you he was here, lying right here on the floor."

"What sort of a suit was he wearing?" Richard asked.

"Darkish." Miss Violet's eyes were wide and scared.

Richard nodded. "I'll look around. He might have crawled off somewhere."

Doc Paunders lowered himself into an armchair and grunted. "All right, haul out the cookies and sherry. It's a pity you girls couldn't learn how to make coffee and a man-sized pie."

"We should hardly be inspired to learn on your account," Miss Ivy sniffed.

"We haven't any pie," Miss Violet said vaguely. "I'll bring the cookies. I want to see what Richard's doing. We're drinking a toast tonight, you know. We couldn't get you on the phone, Doctor, so I expect you haven't heard about it yet."

Richard had gone first to the kitchen, and then back to the front hall, and up the stairs. There were two bedrooms, front and back, at one side of the house, and on the other, the stairs, hall and bathroom. He searched the rooms carefully and found nothing and became conscious of a faint sense of guilt. It seemed as though they might be having hallucinations now, and probably it was all his fault. Getting them excited and upset because he lost his temper and tried to get even with Ada. He'd have to explain to her and apologize, and then tell his aunts that the wedding was off.

There was a telephone in the upstairs hall, and he picked it up and put through a call to Ada. She answered immediately and asked, "What about the dead man? Who is he?"

"No man. Overexcited imagination, maybe."

"Oh."

"Look, Ada, I'm sorry about tonight. I lost my temper when I saw that announcement in the paper. I knew you were using the thing for some purpose of your own, and I'll admit it made me sore. But I realize I shouldn't have done it, and I'll tell the aunts that the wedding is off, or delayed, or whatever you like."

The phone seemed to chill against his ear as Ada said, "Oh, no. Don't tell them that the wedding's off, because it is not. You let your temper out one notch too far when you mentioned a date. I shall see you tomorrow at eleven for the license. Good night."

Richard replaced the phone slowly and stared at nothing. Was she trying to scare him, or was she planning to jilt him at the altar for all his friends to see?

He went downstairs, and Miss Ivy said, "Sit down, Richard, do. I presume you found nothing upstairs?"

Richard shook his head and asked suddenly, "By the way, where are you putting the altar?"

Doc Paunders halted a cookie halfway to his mouth, and Miss Violet said eagerly, "In the dining room, dear. That little lowboy, all banked with white flowers, and we shall bring down the two large silver candelabra."

Doc Paunders looked bewildered. "What is this? Are you fixing a funeral for that body that got away?"

Miss Ivy explained briefly, and dutifully invited him to the wedding.

He scratched his chin and shifted his weight in the armchair. "Seems a bit, er—"

"What?"

"Well— You mean you're going to run a wedding right over *him?*"

Miss Violet drew breath in a little gasp, but Miss Ivy said firmly, "He changed a little before he died. He said once that he thought perhaps Richard was *all* Balron, and as such, he felt quite kindly towards him."

"But the girl?"

"He never knew her," Miss Violet said quickly. "If he had, he'd have loved her, as we all do."

Doc Paunders shook his head. "Maybe I'm superstitious, but you wouldn't get me to put on the noose over somebody's grave. Why don't you go up to the big house?"

"There's no time," Miss Ivy said impatiently. "And I simply cannot see what earthly difference it makes, having it over Father's grave. It would be downright silly at the big house, anyway, since we're having very few guests."

"Who's going to be here?" Richard asked.

Miss Ivy counted on her fingers. "Miss Dedingham and Mr. Hernand, of course. Doctor, here, and the judge."

"How about my mother?"

There was a slight pause, and then Miss Violet said gently, "Now, dear, I don't think she'd want to come. She's such a *busy* person."

Miss Ivy heaved a sharp little sigh. "Don't be absurd, Violet. I'll phone her in the morning."

"Tonight," Richard said flatly.

"Why don't you ask her yourself?"

"It's your house."

The phone rang, and Doc Paunders stretched an arm for it. He said, "Hello," and "Yes," and handed it over to Richard. "Speak of the devil," he observed cheerfully.

Richard said, "Hello," and his mother's voice trilled into his ear. When he could break in he said loudly, "We were just going to phone you, to invite you to my wedding tomorrow."

"Who's 'we'?"

"Aunt Ivy and myself."

"You don't say! What about that halfwit, Violet?"

"Probably not," Richard murmured.

"If you promise to have her on a leash, I'll be there in my best hat. And listen, what about the dead man?"

"Not here."

Mrs. Balron laughed. "Probably asked Grandpa to move over downstairs. I always said no decent male would want to be caught dead around that pair." She hung up, and Richard went back to his chair.

He had noticed a small object lying under the table, and he stooped and picked it up.

It was a bullet.

8

"What is it?" Miss Ivy asked in an annoyed voice.

Richard held it up. "It's a bullet, from one of your guns, no doubt."

"Any bullets we may have are kept where they belong," Miss Ivy said coldly. "We don't throw them on the floor."

"Nonsense." Doc Paunders reached for another cookie. "You girls never were tidy."

Miss Violet fluttered up and said, "Give it to me. I'll put it away."

Richard slipped the bullet into his pocket. "I'll keep it for the time being."

"That's right where the dead man was lying," Miss Violet whimpered. "Where you picked it up, I mean. I won't be able to sleep tonight, I know I won't. I'm scared. He—he must be walking."

"Now look," Richard said sensibly. "You're all upset and bothered. I don't believe you saw a man at all, just shadows, and in your excited state—"

"No." Miss Ivy spoke quietly enough, but her fingers tapped with a clicking sound on the table. "There *was* a man, and he may come back. Perhaps he wasn't dead."

"Boiled to the eyebrows, maybe," Doc Paunders suggested comfortably.

Richard sighed. "I should be enjoying my bachelor dinner tonight, but I'll stay here and guard you."

Miss Ivy's fingers ceased their tattoo, and she relaxed back into her chair. "I shan't pretend that I am not relieved. Thank you, Richard. You can sleep on the couch here. I'm sure you'll be quite comfortable."

Richard gave the couch a glum look, and Doc Paunders stood up and shook down his trousers. "I'll be getting along, then, since you haven't any bodies for me."

"I'll drop you home," Richard said.

"Oh no you won't. One ride in that electric funeral coach is enough."

Richard nodded. "My car is still parked downtown. I'll walk with you and get it."

"Are you leaving us here alone?" Miss Violet quavered.

"I won't be long," Richard assured her. "Lock the doors while I'm gone. You'll be all right."

Miss Ivy stood up. "Very well. Knock three times when you get back."

Richard found that he was cold without his coat, and he had mislaid his hat somewhere, since he was so unused to wearing one. Doc Paunders protested breathlessly several times at the pace he was setting.

He picked up the car and decided to drive home for some clothes and his topcoat. As he came into the lower hall Mrs. Balron called from upstairs, "That you, Richard?"

"No," he said, "I'm a burglar."

She leaned over the banister. "What on earth made you decide to get married tomorrow?"

"Why not? One day is much like another."

"But such a rush—it's almost indecent. Madge phoned me, and she was all confused. Said that everybody was talking about the wedding tomorrow."

"I'm spending the night with the aunts," Richard said. "They're afraid the dead man might return."

"Oh. And I suppose your poor old mother can battle for herself if he decides to walk in here on his stiffening legs."

"If he's considering tackling you, someone ought to warn him."

"Oh, be quiet! Where are you spending your honeymoon?"

Richard had been moving around his room, and he stopped with his pajama pants in one hand and his toothbrush in the other. "Hmm. That's a fine thing, isn't it? I have to be in court early the next morning. Looks as though we'll have to spend our honeymoon in the hotel."

"If I'd had several children," Mrs. Balron said thoughtfully, "there might have been one with a brain. What sort of a ring did you buy her?"

"I'm going to use a cigar band."

Mrs. Balron squinted at him. "You're not fooling me, you know. You went around there in one of your fiendish tempers and threatened her, and she called your bluff."

Richard had his head in the closet, and he said in a muffled voice, "That's a bit obscure. What would I threaten her with?"

"Marriage, I suppose, and she called you. Why wouldn't she, you goof? A man with—"

"A yellow convertible."

Mrs. Balron sniffed. "What time is the wedding?"

"Four o'clock, I think, or it may be five."

"Well, you'd better find out. I'd look silly getting there an hour too soon, but on the other hand, I don't want to miss the sight of you standing up and plighting your troth."

"Come at four," Richard said, emerging from the closet. "If you find you're too early, you can lurk in the bushes."

"I'm going with you," Mrs. Balron declared firmly. "I'm the mother of the groom. I'll have to fly out in the morning and get a dress, too, and a hat."

"Make it something quiet, will you? None of your bright reds. I'm wearing my blue, and I don't want to be put in the shade, so be careful. Well, I'm off. Good night."

She followed him down the stairs and said crossly, "I don't see why you have to go over there. What's one dead man, more or less? They have a dead man in the cellar all the time."

"He's had the grace to stay where they put him. Lock the door after me, and go to bed. I'll bring the car back in the morning."

The aunts were waiting for him when he got back to their house, and they had made up the couch with sheets and a blanket. They said good night almost immediately and went upstairs, and Richard measured himself briefly on the couch. It was inches too short, and he got up again, shrugging. He did not undress at once, but went to the small chest of drawers where he had found the revolvers. They had been removed, and he swore softly. He was determined to find them and extract the bullets, even though they could get more.

He went through all the drawers in the little parlor and dining room without result. He moved on to the kitchen, but was discouraged by the confusion that Annie had left behind her. He wondered how she managed to produce breakfast out of that mess, and was turning away when his eye fell on the door to the cellar. Might as well go down and have another look at that hole, Annie's new grave. Perhaps he could discover some reason for it. In any case, he'd speak to his aunts about it in the morning.

He tried the back-door key first, and it turned the lock quite easily. He had to fumble a little for the light switch, but he found it presently and turned it on. He descended to stillness and surveyed again the imposing tomb of his grandfather. Hideous, expensive, and gruesome. Why on earth were people so concerned about the final disposal of their bones?

He turned away and went to the side where he had found the excavation. He pried up the linoleum and the wood and peered in, and was startled into a smothered exclamation. There was something lying at the bottom now, covered with a piece of canvas. His forehead was beaded with perspiration, and he shook his head irritably. Whatever was there was not big enough to be a body. Why should be assume that this was a grave merely because of Annie's macabre speculations?

He dropped flat onto the linoleum and, reaching an arm, pulled gingerly at the dusty canvas. It had been used to cover several newspaper-wrapped packages, and he hauled them out, one by one. He sat back and opened them and found himself completely bewildered. A pitcher, three wineglasses, a brass lamp, an ornate clock. What *was* it? Could one of the aunts have gone quite batty? Or both of them? What else?

He replaced everything exactly as he had found it and stood up, brushing vaguely at his trousers. Well, no use hanging around here. Might as well go up and dangle his feet over the end of the couch.

He walked to the stairs and shook his head again over the linoleum. Certainly was a lousy job—sooner or later it would rot away with water seeping up under it. He must remember to ask his aunts who had done it. They ought to sue him, whoever he was.

He returned to the kitchen and shut and locked the cellar door behind him, and then went along to the parlor. He pulled out a cigarette and fumbled impatiently for his lighter until it dawned on him that it was no longer in his pocket. He considered for a moment, and then sighed. It had fallen out when he stooped down to the excavation, of course. He'd dropped it that way before—and would continue to drop it that way until he had sense enough to change it to another pocket.

He went back to the kitchen, unlocked the cellar door, and switched on the light, and then stood very still at the top of the stairs. Something was rustling down there, or someone walking very quietly. He felt his heart move into a quicker beat, and he set his jaw. He was behaving as foolishly as the aunts. This lousy little bandbox of a house was full of odd noises. No one was down there except the old man, properly entombed. There was no outside door to the cellar. He stood at the only entrance, and the stained-glass windows had been securely nailed into their frames. There was no way of opening them.

He went down, setting his feet firmly on the steps. There was no one there, of course, and nothing, except his lighter, lying on the floor. He picked it up and slipped it into a deeper pocket, and then went around and examined the windows. There were three of them, and they were unbroken, and showed no signs of tampering.

So it was just the noises of an old house that he had heard, nothing more. No wonder some of these old places had the reputation of being haunted.

He climbed to the kitchen again, turned off the cellar light, and locked the door. He was careful to return the key to the back door, and then he stood for a moment, his eyes roaming in search of coffee. He felt that he needed something, and he didn't expect to get much sleep, anyway.

It took some time to assemble the equipment, but at last he had a brew over the lighted gas, and while it heated he decided to return to the tiny parlor and prowl through the drawers of the little chest again. He did a more thorough job of searching this time, and discovered that the revolvers had been put in a box and buried beneath a froth of lace doilies. He drew it out and put it on the table. At least he would unload the guns, for what good it might do. He extracted the single bullet from each, and looked at them as they lay on the palm of his hand.

He could see at once that there was a difference. He nudged them with a careful finger, and realized that one was a blank.

9

He had separated the guns, and remembered that the blank had come from the one at his right hand. They appeared to be the same—he could find no difference—and he wondered whether that was the way they played it. Just one bullet in one of the guns, and they mixed them up. But, why the blank? It would explain the misses. A bang, and nobody dead. On the other hand, if they had missed with real bullets, there should be holes in the wall.

He got up and gave the walls a brief inspection, but found nothing. He realized that it would take a long, minute survey before he could be sure that there were no holes, and he gave it up with a shrug and returned to the revolvers. He wanted to make some sort of tiny mark on one of them so that he could tell them apart, and he decided to put a small scratch on the end of the handle. He lifted one of the guns and turned it over, and then sat staring. It had already been done, just a small I scratched at the end. He picked up the other one and found a V. So it was Violet's gun which had had the live bullet, and Ivy's the blank.

He knew that Violet was a weaker character than Ivy, but he couldn't see her doing a thing like this. It would be murder, really. She was protected, and poor Ivy was right out in the open. Violet had missed several times, and there was one way of finding out whether her misses had been with live bullets, or with blanks. He'd have to search every inch of the room. Too big a job for tonight, and he was too tired. He gave the couch a glance of disfavor, and then heard the coffee sputtering over onto the stove.

He hurried to the kitchen and surveyed the mess a little ruefully. Oh well, it didn't really matter. Annie's method was to stack the dishes and sweep the crumbs under the sink, and his aunts never soiled their fingers with menial work. He supposed that they ate cookies and drank sherry on Annie's day off and lined the glasses and little plates up on the drainboard. He foraged for food, and found only raisin bread and cream cheese. It would not have been his choice, but he munched hungrily at it while he drank his coffee.

The refreshment gave him a lift, and he decided to tackle the job of a thorough search for bullet holes at once. He was thinking of Ada as he returned to the parlor, and he wondered what was in her mind. Was she planning to jilt him at the altar, make him look a fool in his home town? It would create quite a sensation, at that, the town's most eligible bachelor left standing before the lowboy in the dining room. He grinned to himself and pictured his mother, in her new dress and hat, relieving her mind on the subject.

He started his search of the parlor and did it so thoroughly that it took him two hours. He took one break for more coffee, but otherwise stuck doggedly to the job, and was able to satisfy himself completely that all his aunts' misses had been with blanks. There were no marks anywhere on the walls, floors, ceilings, or furniture in the hall, parlor, and dining room. He did not bother with the kitchen since he knew that his aunts considered it an apartment to be viewed through a lorgnette, if at all.

He was very tired now, and after another unfavorable glance at the couch he hauled the sheets, blanket, and a pillow onto the floor, and stretched out with his head under the table and his feet nudging uneasily at a chair. In spite of his fatigue, it was some time before he slept, and when he did drowse off at last it was to the blurred sensation of a dead man lying beside him, while his mind wearily defended Violet against the ugly implication of the blank bullet.

It seemed only minutes before he was awakened by a yell from Annie. She had come in at six o'clock to get an early start on cleaning up for the wedding. Richard tried to move and was conscious of pain in every part of his body. He groaned loudly and muttered, "This is what soft living has done for me."

Annie had recognized him, and regained her composure. She surveyed him with hands on hips. "You call that soft, living with *your* ma?"

One of the aunts called from upstairs, "Annie! What is it? What has happened?"

Richard did not wait even for a cup of coffee. He stumbled out to his car, drove straight home, and crept in without waking his mother. He went to bed and to sleep.

Mrs. Balron woke him at ten. She dumped a breakfast tray onto his lap, raised the blind with a loud clatter, and said cheerfully, "Happy the groom the sun shines on. When did you get in? I didn't hear you."

Richard eased his sore muscles and moaned, "Ten o'clock! How am I going to get through all the work I have to do?"

"Who cares?" said Mrs. Balron. "Mrs. Evans has been on the phone from time to time, clucking away as usual. I told her to close the joint and come on out to the wedding."

"What did she say?" Richard asked, trying to pour coffee while the tray wobbled on his knees.

"Said she couldn't understand why you didn't postpone your wedding until the weekend. Seems you're going to be much too busy to get married today. She doesn't know how you'll wedge it in."

"To which you replied?"

"I told her that once in a while, just for practice, she ought to remember that you're the boss and she's the office worker."

"Yeah?"

"Yes, but you can't shut that woman up. She said there wouldn't be an office for her to work in if she allowed herself to remember things like that."

"You didn't hang up like a sissy at that point, did you?"

"Certainly not!" said Mrs. Balron emphatically. "I asked her just what she thought she was insinuating."

Richard disappeared silently behind his coffee cup, and his mother walked to the mirror and patted her hair. "The woman has some nerve! She said she wasn't insinuating, she was telling me straight, that you would never get to any appointment, anywhere, if she wasn't there to speed you on your way. I would have singed her ear, but before I could say anything she backed up and apologized."

"Mrs. Evans apologized?"

"Yes. As good as, anyway. She said she loved my new coat, and of course that meant she was sorry for what she'd said and hoped I wasn't mad."

"Ah yes." Richard put the tray aside. "Would you be good enough to hop it? I want to shower and dress."

He was breathless by the time he arrived at his office, and Mrs. Evans was distinctly acid. "I don't know how you plan to get it all done, Mr. Balron. It's just on eleven now."

He worked feverishly for an hour before the telephone interrupted him. It was Ada, and she asked coldly, "Why aren't you here?"

"I'm sorry, I've been very busy. Did you, er, expect me for lunch?"

"I expected you to keep an appointment that you made with me last night. Eleven o'clock, to get our marriage license."

"License? Oh. Yes. Well, look, I should have phoned you earlier, of course. You see you have to wait three days after getting the license before you can use it, and then— I'm terribly rushed today. I have to be in court in the morning—"

"You mean we can't be married today?"

"Well, no, I'm afraid not. I mean, the license—three days—"

"Have you phoned the aunts, or anyone else, to say that the wedding is off? Are you allowing them to go on with all those expensive arrangements for nothing?"

"Not at all," Richard said stiffly. "They'll enjoy the party, and so will I. I'll be able to be there for about twenty minutes. Then I'll foot the bill, and we'll explain."

"Oh no." She gave a soft little laugh. "You are going through with this, Richard. It was not my suggestion, but yours. And the license won't save you. Judge Meeklyn has made a special arrangement for us, and you can sign when you get to the aunts' house. He tells me that you are busy today, so you'd better get back to your work, but you will show up for your wedding at the aunts' at four o'clock, or I'll sue you for everything you own."

Richard was startled back to his surroundings when Mrs. Evans took the phone, still dangling in his hand, and replaced it in its cradle. "Bad news?" she asked briskly.

He glanced at her and dropped his eyes without answering. The woman was being corny. She knew perfectly well that he had been talking to Ada, and what he had said. She merely wanted a statement so that she could quote.

He tried to get back to his work, but at one o'clock he gave up entirely and told Mrs. Evans that he was going out for a bite to eat. She nodded and observed, quite politely, that she was hungry too, but would not have time for lunch. Richard, equally courteous, promised to send in coffee and a sandwich.

He drove to an eating place out of town because he wanted to think. He couldn't blame Ada for wanting to punish his bad temper, but surely the gag had gone far enough. Marriage was serious. But not to Ada, evidently. Well, she was involved with something, probably someone's husband, and she would feel nicely protected if she were newly married. It would supposedly take the wife off her neck. The point was, ought he to let Ada get away with it? She'd threatened to sue him. Breach of promise? With the whole town to back her up. Oh, she'd never go that far. Or would she? He could fight, but he knew he wouldn't, if she really wanted to marry him. As a matter of fact, he liked the thought of marrying Ada, but he had never been able to convince himself that it would work out. He had his living here, and she could never settle down in a small town. Anyway, if she had made up her mind, let her marry him and then divorce him. It didn't really matter.

On the way back he was stopped by a red light in a small village. His eyes strayed idly as he waited, and came to rest on the front window of a cottage that stood almost flush with the street. A neat sign proclaimed "Antiques," and arranged directly under the sign was his aunts' best china tea set.

10

Richard pulled off the road and got out of his car. He went over to the window and carefully inspected the display of china—and decided that there could be no mistake. This was his aunts' lavender and gold tea set. In his memory they had never used it, and it was kept in a glass-fronted cabinet as the main attraction, although they'd had other bits of china grouped around it.

He went inside and was confronted by a tall, vague woman who kept replacing a stubbornly escaping wisp of hair. She gave him the price of the tea set, which staggered him, and he put his hands firmly into his pockets. He'd be damned if he'd buy it back for them. He asked where she had got it, but she set her pale lips and informed him that she never revealed the sources of her supply.

He returned to his car, and a glance at his watch showed him that it was after two. He swung out onto the highway in a bit of a hurry, but his thoughts were on the aunts. They were not short of money.

Each had her private income, and they shared expenses. But those things in the cellar must be destined for the antique shop, too, and why? Had they gone nuts? Digging a big hole in the cellar and hiding the stuff there before selling it was not normal behavior. No, someone else was stealing things, and they hid the stuff first to find out whether the aunts would miss it. Annie? She would hardly tell him about the hole if she had dug it herself. Perhaps the thieving and the hole were two different projects. Must be. The tea set had come from the big house, and probably the other things as well, so why would anybody dig a hole for them at the little house? In any case, the hole was too big for such small articles. He was conscious of a sudden proprietary anger that was unfamiliar. All those things pilfered, and God knows what else. A moment later he laughed at himself. The things were not his, even though he was to be installed as master at the big house, but he must speak to his aunts about it without delay.

It was after three when he got home, and his mother met him at the door.

"Where in the name of heaven have you been? Everyone is looking for you, and Ada is practically resigned to being jilted."

"She hopes," Richard said grimly. "Nothing doing. Have you laid out my Sunday clothes?"

"Since when have I laid out clothes for you?"

"I can't remember that you ever did," Richard admitted. "But I thought on my wedding day—"

"It's just as well I never went in for that sort of foolishness," Mrs. Balron assured him. "You're marrying a girl who's had no one to think about but herself. You'll really be doing housework now, and you'll have to wait on *her*. In fact, you'll be glad when she goes on tour so that you can get a rest."

"What does a groom wear for a four-o'clock wedding?" Richard asked. "Would I be expected to hang tails on my back at that hour?"

"You haven't any tails."

"Go and get yourself dressed," Richard said, "and then come back and help me with the finishing touches."

As it happened, he was ready first and was obliged to give his mother help with her own finishing touches. He rushed her out of the house and into the car, where she settled her hat and observed that she felt silly without a corsage, and her the mother of the groom. Richard made no reply, but he was conscious of an uneasy sense of guilt. The groom was supposed to supply flowers all around, wasn't he? Including a buttonhole for himself. Oh, well. They'd all look silly.

"A corsage is a small matter," he said, squinting into the sun, "but how am I going to look without a best man? I wonder if Johnny's at home. I could stop and pick him up."

"Johnny is not at home. He's on his way to the wedding, or already there. I told him. Maybe I don't waste my time laying out your clothes, but at least I see to the important things. I wouldn't let you get married without a best man to hold your hand."

Richard turned into his aunts' street and found both curbs lined with cars. He tried to drop his mother at the front door, but she refused to move. "Get going and park the thing. I'm staying with you, no matter how far I have to walk. You know very well I'd be found lying on the path with my throat cut if I tried to get in there by myself."

"All right." He cruised on down the road. "Now, listen. Try and behave yourself, at least during the ceremony, will you? Don't snicker, and don't make any *sotto voce* snide remarks."

Mrs. Balron got out of the car, and waved to Mr. Hernand, who was approaching from the direction of his house. He wore a hat but no topcoat, which was usual. He always said that going without a hat courted pneumonia, and affirmed with equal vehemence that none but sissies coddled themselves in extra coats.

"Well, Richard, this is quite a surprise to all of us, getting married so suddenly."

"Have to get married some time," Richard muttered, eying the car and wondering whether it was close enough to the curb.

"Why?"

"So that he won't be an old maid like you," Mrs. Balron explained kindly.

Mr. Hernand told her, in an offended voice, that there were a lot of girls that he could have had if he'd wanted them, and added, "Remember when *you* were trying to make up to me?"

Mrs. Balron stopped dead and put a hand to her heart. "There are some lies that are just right out beyond the pale. I think I'm going to have a stroke."

Richard took her arm and hustled her up the path to the house. He had a struggle to get the door open, and he wedged his way in, still hanging on to his mother, while Mr. Hernand pushed from behind. They got in, but that was all. The hall was jammed with people, and Mr. Hernand could not get in far enough to close the door behind him. Richard saw his predicament and shoved doggedly until Mr. Hernand's outer proportions were eased inside and the door closed.

"What is it?" Richard whispered. "They told me they were having only five or six people."

"Gate crashers," Mrs. Balron said happily. "Makes a better party, doesn't it? Shows how popular you are, too."

Someone caught sight of Richard and called, "Here's the groom! Hey, Johnny, here he is!"

Johnny Smith appeared at once and dragged Richard away through the crowd. Mrs. Balron followed for a short distance in the opening they made, but lost them somewhere in the parlor. She found herself squashed up against a chair on which Miss Dedingham sat with folded hands.

They regarded each other without warmth, and Miss Dedingham murmured, "You're the mother of the groom, are you not?"

"No use denying it," said Mrs. Balron. "I apologize, of course."

Miss Dedingham coughed. "He's a nice boy, but I hate to see him marry a common actress."

"History repeats itself," said Mrs. Balron airily. "His father was a nice boy too, and he married a common clerk."

Miss Dedingham stared. "Well, but I understood your people were poor but honest."

Mrs. Balron shook her head. "Gossip is always distorted, isn't it? My people were poor, but far from honest. I could tell you—"

"Hush." Miss Dedingham's face was red. "I believe they are about to begin."

Annie was opening the sliding doors between the parlor and the dining room. She was acting on instructions from Richard, who had been standing in the kitchen with Johnny, Judge Meeklyn, and the minister.

The guests were able to spread into the dining room now, and they made a little aisle from the stairway in the hall through to the lowboy altar in the dining room. Someone began the wedding march on the small piano, and the bridal procession appeared at the head of the stairs.

Miss Ivy and Miss Violet came first, arrayed in their best afternoon gowns. Ada followed alone, looking slender and pretty in a white evening gown and the aunts' veil. She felt as though she were playing a part on the stage, but could have found a better arrangement for her hands if she'd had a bridal bouquet. Miss Violet looked sentimental and happy, but Miss Ivy's face was forbidding. She longed to stop the march and order all the uninvited people out of the house.

Mrs. Balron murmured, "Look at the two dry old sticks trying to pretend they're bridesmaids."

The bridal party rounded the parlor and headed into the dining room, and Richard watched them approach from his spot in front of the altar. Why, he thought, she's actually enjoying herself. How can she be so flip? Making a convenience of marriage, and not worrying about it, either. She looked lovely, of course.

Ada raised her eyes and smiled, and Richard ran a finger around the inside of his collar. It was hot in this small, stuffy place, and his aunts were nuts. So was he, to let this thing go through.

The minister cleared his throat, and the ceremony was on. At its conclusion, Ada and Richard faced the crowd with an aunt on each side, and Annie came in with sherry and cookies. When Mrs. Balron appeared in the line of those offering congratulations she kissed Ada, and then said in a loud, clear voice, "I hope you'll be happy, son, but there's always the divorce court if it doesn't work out. So nice of your aunts to invite me to your wedding. They can have the place cleaned out thoroughly tomorrow, and no harm done."

Miss Ivy and Miss Violet gazed over her head. They were shaking hands with only a few of the people who passed by.

Everyone seemed to be having a good time. Champagne was served, but there was not enough to go around, and a neat, white wedding cake was eaten to the last crumb when the cookies ran out.

Mrs. Balron moved over to Richard and said amiably, "I never realized you were so stingy. No flowers for the bridesmaids, and not even a bridal bouquet."

Richard glanced at Ada's empty hands and at the diamond wedding band she wore, which had belonged to her mother.

Mrs. Balron nudged him. "Too late now. Listen, do you know the police are outside? Seems the old girls have lost their Royal china tea set."

11

Miss Ivy overheard this item, and she said abruptly, "come on, Violet."

The two of them began to fight their way through the crowd, and Richard called after them, but they did not hear him. He said "Excuse me" to Ada and followed them as fast as he could.

Out on the front porch, hunching their shoulders in the chilly wind, the sisters were confronting a policeman. "A tea set is missing from our house, the big house," Miss Ivy said crisply. "We intended to use it today, but it's just as well, perhaps, that we could not find it. Something would surely have been broken, with all that vulgar crowd. However, it has been stolen, and you must find it. There will be a reward."

"Wait a minute," Richard broke in. "I know where it is. I saw it." He explained while the policeman wrote busily, and the aunts shook their heads and made little sounds of annoyance. The policeman presently made off to recapture the tea set, and Richard turned to go back into the house.

Miss Ivy held him with a hand on his arm. "Richard, you are really in a daze, my dear. You sent no flowers. Of course I blame your mother. She should have seen to it. Now, what arrangements have you made for the honeymoon?"

"Well, I—I haven't made any, as a matter of fact."

Miss Ivy frowned and said, "Tsk!" and Miss Violet cried, "Poor little Ada! It's a shame!"

"We'll go somewhere later," Richard said defensively. "I'm very busy just now. Have to be in court in the morning."

"Of course, dear, we quite understand." Miss Ivy sent a quelling glance at Miss Violet. "It works out very well, as it so happens. I've had a part of the big house thoroughly cleaned, and you can go straight there very comfortably. It will relieve my mind to have you living there, because things have been disappearing, and I want you to keep an eye out for the thief."

"But—"

The aunts turned and went into the house, and Richard shrugged. Well, he was married, and he could hardly go home, so why not the big house? Where else?

He went inside, and realized that some of the people must have left, since there was more room to move around. Someone was playing the piano, and Ada was dancing with Johnny, very expertly, with a lot of dipping and swaying. The aunts had stopped and were gazing with obvious disapproval, and Richard waded in and broke it up.

"Come on, Ada, the wedding's over. Get your duds and we'll go home."

"Home?"

He explained about the big house, and she nodded and went upstairs without a word. She was down again in a short time, wearing a smartly tailored suit and topcoat and carrying a suitcase.

Almost everyone had left by this time. The aunts were standing firmly in the middle of the floor so that no one could dance, and most of them had taken the hint and gone off.

Richard and Ada took their leave, accompanied by Miss Dedingham, Doc Paunders, Mr. Hernand, and Judge Meeklyn. Outside, they found that the late guests had congregated on the lawn, and were ready and waiting with handfuls of rice and confetti. Richard took Ada's arm and hurried her through the storm to his car.

"I have to go to the hotel and check out, and I've another bag there," Ada said. She added after a moment, "What on earth's that noise?"

Richard stopped the car, got out, and went around to the back, and presently returned exhibiting three tin cans and an old shoe. He threw them into the gutter and climbed in again.

"I suppose you have to pick up a bag too?" Ada asked.

He nodded. "I'll take you to the hotel first."

He was late in calling back for her. He'd had to run out and buy a new car. Mrs. Balron couldn't bring herself to give up the yellow convertible, and said so.

"You run on down to Jake's," she told him. "He's home by now, but he'll manage it for you. He has that sedan left, and the new cars are in, so he'll make a price for you. I'll help you pay for it. I'll buy this one, and pay you, let's see, fifteen dollars a month until it's all cleared off."

"How long do you expect to live?" Richard asked.

"That yellow convertible is a secondhand job," Mrs. Balron said coldly. "I'll pay you fifteen a month for a year, and I don't want to hear any more about it. You go and see Jake, and pick up the blue sedan."

"I do not like blue."

"Get going," said Mrs. Balron with finality. "I'll pack for you and have your suitcase ready when you get back."

Richard called for Ada at the hotel in his new, small, blue sedan, and they drove off to the big house in almost total silence. When they arrived he brought the baggage in from the car and put it down in the spacious front hall.

"When did you last eat?" Ada asked.

"I can't remember."

"Well"—she put her little finger between her teeth, and chewed thoughtfully—"we should have gone out somewhere, I suppose, but perhaps they left something in the refrigerator."

"I'll take you out," he said, but she was already heading for the kitchen and he followed.

The kitchen was huge, and Ada pattered across gleaming lino-leum to a tall, white refrigerator. She swung the door wide and nod-ded in satisfaction. "It's all right. They've stocked us up."

Richard sat down on a chair and watched her curiously. After a moment he said, "Now that it's all over, do you mind telling me why you did it?"

She glanced at him with a half smile. "It's your own fault. I was in a spot, and here you came in, ranting and raving, and saying through your clenched teeth that we were going to be married. It suited me to go through with it, and it serves you right. This is one time you'll have to pay full price for that lousy temper of yours."

"Not at all." Richard grinned at her. "I like being married to you. The point is how are you going to like it?"

Ada turned from the long, streamlined, white range and looked full at him. "I don't know, and you don't either. We can find ou. In other words, we can go steady for a while and see whether we'd like to be married. If we decide against it, we can get a divorce."

"Go steady?" Richard rumpled his hair. "You mean I have to date you often, whether I want to or not?"

She turned back to the stove and said mildly, "Divorce is expensive. You might try dating me often, and see how we both feel about it."

"But you won't be here to date the day after tomorrow."

"Yes, I'll be here." Ada drew a long breath that might have been a sigh. "I've decided to give up that part. I'm sick and tired of putting on a bright smile for nasty old men. I shall play the lady of the manor for a while and see how I like it." She added, "What happened to the yellow convertible? That little blue thing is corny, and doesn't fit our status."

"You're hurting my feelings. I bought that as a wedding present for you. You see, Mother—"

"Oh." Ada nodded. "I'll take the blue around to your mother tomorrow and get the yellow back."

"Are you going to drive me to work first?" he asked. "Because if not, you'll have to get up at five-thirty to get my breakfast. It's a long walk to the office from here."

"Details," said Ada absently. "Will you kindly take yourself off somewhere while I finish this dinner? I'll call you."

Richard wandered out of the back door and into the yard. He saw Pat working in a flower bed a short distance away, and sauntered in that direction.

Pat straightened up, pushed an ancient hat to the back of his head, and began immediately to complain.

"I don't know what them two old wimmin think I am. Look at these here grounds, acres, and I got to keep the whole thing lookin' good, or it's nag, nag, nag from both of them, or anyways, especially Miss Ivy. It ain't enough to keep the grass tidy, but they got to have flowers, too, all the way from March to November. You ever hear the beat of that? It's good their eyes is dimmed, some, so they can't see all them paper blooms ain't real."

"Paper blooms?"

Pat scratched his head vigorously. "They're easy fooled. If there ain't no flowers, they think I been loafing, so bits of colored paper stuck on the stalks ain't so much fuss, and everybody feels good."

"You're a crook," Richard said, laughing at him.

"I been working since dawn broke," Pat said accusingly. "They come rushin' over here, yappin' about the bride and groom, and how I got to have the grounds all spit and polish. I'm tellin' you now, I just ain't had the time to do it, nor no one could." He added querulously, "I don't see what possessed you to stumble over your feet gettin' married in such a hurry."

"I didn't stumble over my feet."

Pat viewed the garden for a moment of silence, and then asked, "You got any black tissue paper?"

"What?"

"Black tissue paper."

"What for?"

"They want them black iris bloomin' now. Not later, mind you, when they will bloom, but now. Miss Ivy told me, and there ain't no use tryin' to argue, because she don't listen. The iris don't listen, neither, so I got to have some black tissue paper."

"It's rank fraud," Richard said, "but you're an old retainer, so I'll bring you some carbon paper from the office."

Ada called from the kitchen door, and he turned away and walked back. He went in and asked, "Dinner ready?"

"No, but it's time to mix the cocktails, and you'll have to do that. Take them to the living room, and I'll be there shortly."

Richard remembered that the old man had kept his liquor in the cellar, and he went down. He was a little surprised at the size of the collection, hundreds of bottles in great variety. His aunts drank only wine, of course, but he wondered at the thief who had carried away a tea set and left this array undisturbed. He took gin and dry vermouth and went upstairs again.

He found Ada sitting in an armchair in the library. She had changed to a dark green hostess gown, and was smoking a cigarette. "That living room, or drawing room, or whatever they call it, is the last word in elegance, but just two people are apt to get lost there. More comfortable to have our cocktails here."

She had set a match to the log fire, and Richard put his tray onto a table and rubbed his hands with a feeling of well-being. "We're celebrating, eh?"

"Celebrating?"

"Cocktails, and you in that fancy gown."

"I change into a gown and have cocktails every night before dinner."

"You'll have to forgive me," Richard murmured. "I'm just a hick. I usually come in and set at the kitchen table in my overalls."

"Pour me a cocktail and hand it to me."

Richard poured her a cocktail and handed it to her.

Suddenly there were sounds of emergency in the hall, and then Annie rushed into the room.

"Mr. Richard, you must come right away. Those two old sisters are fighting something terrible."

12

Richard put down his cocktail glass, grimaced at Ada, and followed Annie out. They hurried down the long driveway together, and over to the little house, where they went in at the back door. Annie remained in the kitchen and gestured with her thumb, and Richard went to the parlor.

The Misses Balron were seated quietly in their favorite chairs, Miss Ivy reading, and Miss Violet working at her embroidery. They raised surprised faces to Richard and waited for him to speak.

He sat down and pulled out a cigarette. "What are you two fighting about now?"

Miss Ivy raised her eyebrows and said coldly, "We are not fighting."

Miss Violet dropped the embroidery into her lap. "Why, no."

"You were. I suppose you have it ironed out for the time being, but you had Annie frightened out of her wits, so it must have been bad."

"Annie's wits," said Miss Ivy, "are easily scattered, being few. She must learn to mind her own business. We had an argument, yes, but it has been settled."

"What about?"

"That is our concern, Richard."

Miss Violet said, "Yes, it is," in a child's voice.

"Who won the argument?"

Miss Violet's little mouth pushed out in a pout and she said, "Nobody won it."

"It's nothing." Miss Ivy brushed it away with an impatient gesture. "I'll thank you to attend to your own affairs, Richard."

He looked them over for a moment of silence and shook his head. "You have me worried all the time—the pair of you. Will you consent to live apart?"

"Certainly not," said Miss Ivy flatly.

"It would be much better for both of you."

Miss Violet's small hands hovered over the embroidery in her lap. "Richard, you should really be with your pretty little bride, dear. It isn't nice to leave her alone."

Richard took a long breath and stood up abruptly. "All right, you win. I'll get back to my pretty little bride. Good night."

They both said, "Good night," primly, and Richard retired to the kitchen. Annie looked up, and he put a finger to his lips, and then went and opened the door and closed it with a bang. Annie winked at him, and he nodded and crept back into the hall. But there was no sound from the aunts. They exchanged no word until Annie rang a tinkling bell from somewhere in the back, and then he heard them rustling to their feet. It was Miss Ivy who spoke first. She said, "Six times, then we'll know."

Miss Violet said, "Yes."

They went into the dining room, and Richard returned noiselessly to the kitchen. He put his lips to Annie's ear and whispered, "Can you close the doors between the dining room and parlor? I want to get into the parlor, and I don't want them to see me."

She nodded and replied from the corner of her mouth, "Yeah, I'll say there's a draft."

She went into the dining room, and presently returned and whispered, "O.K."

Richard went to the parlor on the tips of his toes and carefully opened the drawer where the revolvers were kept. He removed the one bullet, but left the blank, and thought grimly that if Miss Ivy had referred to a shooting spree when she said, "six times," at least no one would be killed. He wished that he had another blank for the other revolver, but he didn't, and that was that. He searched quietly through the other drawers, but found nothing more.

He asked Annie, still in a whisper, if she knew what they had been fighting about, but she shook her head. "They was mad as hornets and yelling their heads off, and I couldn't make out most of what they was saying. Something about those there chairs they got, Miss Ivy bellering that their old man woulda been mad, and Miss Violet screechin', 'Father would have approved,' or somethin' like that."

Richard shrugged, and after a moment of indecision he turned and left. He felt a bit aggrieved. He'd gone to the length of this absurd marriage, and still the aunts were battling fiercely.

When he walked into the front hall of the big house he came upon Ada, her slender body drooping against the elaborately carved newel post, her head lowered into her arms. She looked up at him, and he saw that tears had pointed her long lashes.

"Well?" He stopped and stared. "What is it? Did you miss me?"

She brushed her forearm across her eyes in a childish gesture and said, "Oh, shut up! How could I have done such a thing? Marry just anyone because I was in a fury. One of us should have stopped it. It's awful!"

He laughed a little and hung up his coat. "Please! I am not just anyone. I am the biggest catch in this hick town. You shouldn't be upset, you've done very well."

Ada fumbled for a delicate little handkerchief and mopped at her face. "You needn't bother to joke about it. You know as well as I do how awful it is. *One* of us should have had better sense."

"Look, Red." Richard took a step toward her. "I've thought it all out, and there's really only one explanation. We're secretly in love with each other, though we don't admit it, even to ourselves."

She opened her mouth, and he went on quickly, "Don't try to ruin my nice theory by denying it. You *must* admit that if either one of us had really disliked the idea, that one would have stopped the thing, no matter what the circumstances. So let's forget all that part of it. I'll date you, as you suggest, and we'll see whether we like each other. I suppose the dinner has burned away by now?"

Ada restored the little handkerchief to its hiding place on her person and turned toward the kitchen. "I don't think it's too bad. We'll try it."

It was a long way from the front hall to the kitchen, and many steps from the kitchen to the shadowy, paneled dining room. They sat together at one end of the long table and ate with good appetites.

"It's only because we're so hungry, though," Ada said. "It's not much of a meal, actually. You know what I had for lunch?"

"Cookies and sherry?"

She laughed and nodded. "You know, there's a phone here. Madge called."

"Where is the phone? And what did Madge want?"

"The phone is in the hall. I was in the kitchen, but I followed the sound of the bell. I found another room on the way. It looks like a night club."

"A night club? Here?"

"Well, it has little gold chairs and small tables, and a cleared space in the middle, like for dancing."

"Oh." Richard nodded. "That's the salon. They had a highly figured rug there, but it's been stored away. It's valuable. That's where you have the ladies in for afternoon tea."

"Madge, etc."

"Stop looking down your nose," Richard said. "Madge is an important social figure in the town. She is having a party on Saturday to which we are invited."

Ada sighed and stood up. "Get away from the table, will you? I suppose I have to wash these dishes."

Richard gathered plates together and followed her to the kitchen, where they found Annie standing over the stove. She sent an uneasy glance over her shoulder and explained, "I always cook for me and Pat, here, after I get through lookin' after them."

"It's all right," Richard assured her. "You sleep here, don't you?"

"We got rooms over the garage," Annie said more easily. "There's a bathroom there, but there ain't no kitchen. See?"

Richard deposited the dishes he had brought from the dining room and said, "Look here, I'd like to make a deal with you. We'll pay you a regular fee to wash our dishes along with your own. I dislike washing dishes, and it has been my misfortune to have, first, a mother who insisted upon it, and then a wife who tells me that unless I see to it I shall be eating from dirty dishes at the next meal."

Annie swung around from the stove and sent a shocked and reproving glare at Ada, who said lazily, "You should have more faith in me, Annie. I won't start talking like that until I've been married for at least a year."

"It's a wife's place to do the housework," Annie said severely, and added, "Sure I'll wash your dishes, long as you pay."

A bell rang stridently above their heads, and Annie clapped a hand to her heart. When she had recovered she said briefly, "Front door."

Ada and Richard departed for the front hall, and Richard opened the door after a bit of a struggle. Mrs. Evans stood without, looking chilly and withdrawn. He asked her in and introduced her to his bride, but she remained where she was and gave Ada only a disinterested nod.

"I've done what I could on that case for tomorrow," she said, handing Richard a leather briefcase. "I would suggest that you do a little work on it. Otherwise, I don't know what will happen."

"Er, thanks." Richard took the briefcase and shifted his weight from one foot to the other. "Very good of you. Saves me from going down to the office tonight, as I had intended."

Mrs. Evans wore her front hair low on her forehead, and now her eyebrows shifted up under it, disappearing entirely. "You were going to the office *tonight?*"

Richard shifted back to the other foot and said, "Well."

"I'll be off." Mrs. Evans settled her hat. "Had you seen fit to be married over the weekend, I'd have come to your wedding, but congratulations, anyhow."

Richard accompanied her to her car, closed the door on her, and returned to the house, where Ada was waiting for him on the stairs.

"I took your bags up while you were off with Annie," she said. "I fixed a room for you. I'll show you."

He followed her up the stairs and gazed around at the halls and doors on the second floor. "What a house this is! I've never been in it much, you know. It's like a hotel."

Ada nodded. "It's quite a puzzle. A lot of the rooms open into each other, and then, all of a sudden, you'll run into a dead end. I picked out rooms for us at the front. They're across the hall from each other."

She opened the door to a spacious room in which Richard's bags looked a little forlorn. It was a man's room, somber and expensive, with dark mahogany furniture and heavy drapes. He supposed it had been his grandfather's room, and wondered whether he rightly belonged there, what with his mother, and all.

"Mine's right over here," Ada said, "and I'm going to bed. I'm tired. My stupid, smug wrath seems to have died away, and I hope we can make the best of this hideous mistake."

"Isn't 'hideous' a bit strong?" Richard asked mildly.

She said good night and disappeared into her room.

Richard went into his own room, accompanied by a vague sense of guilt. He reflected that, psychiatrically speaking, he ought to sit down and sift these feelings, but he was diverted by the handsome bedroom. Really a fitting place for the gentry, this. He hardly liked to put his modest clothing away in the drawers and cavernous closet, but that was silly. Must be his mother's rakish influence.

He noticed that there was a wind blowing up outside. It had started to whistle and howl around the house. He went to one of the windows and looked out into blackness for a while, and then turned back into the room with a sigh. No use putting it off any longer. He'd have to do some work. He was smiling as he opened the briefcase. If they'd put the wedding off to the weekend, as Mrs. Evans had thought they should, there wouldn't have been a wedding. His smile broadened into a grin. He realized that he was enjoying what Ada called their "hideous mistake."

He sat down to his work and stuck at it grimly for some time. When he found himself getting sleepy he went down to the huge, silent kitchen and made coffee. He found some cake and ate hungrily, wondering idly whether it belonged to Annie and Pat, or to Ada and himself.

The wind was stronger. It crashed and moaned around the house, and he thought that sometimes it sounded like a woman wailing. He shivered and decided to take the rest of the coffee up to his bedroom.

He went back to his work, but he found it increasingly hard to concentrate. The noise of the wind bothered him, and at last he got up and went to a window. He could see nothing, but the wailing sound that rose between the louder crashes was startlingly human. It sounded like a woman, frightened, or in pain.

Suddenly he gripped the drape, and felt moisture on his forehead. It wasn't only wind. He felt sure of it now. Someone was outside, crying and moaning.

13

Richard turned sharply away from the window and went out into the hall. Ada. She was frightened in there, perhaps, of the storm. He went over and rapped on the door.

"What is it?" Ada called. She sounded sleepy.

"Are you all right? I thought I heard you cry out."

"It's only the wind. It woke me up at least twice. Go on back to bed."

"O.K. Good night."

He went back to his room wondering if he had been mistaken. He glanced at the window and saw that it was raining now. Drops spattered against the glass and rolled together in little streams, and the wind howled and whistled as loudly as ever. He went over and drew the shade, and decided that he'd better go to bed and stop imagining things.

He took off his coat and stood holding it, straining his ears. He heard the wail again, unmistakably different from the sound of the wind. A cry of pain or fear—human. And it was somewhere outside the house.

He hastily pulled his coat on again and went out into the hall and quietly down the stairs. He hesitated at the bottom, and then went on to the kitchen in the hope that Pat kept a raincoat hanging around there somewhere. He searched briefly, but could not find anything of the sort, and at last he turned up his coat collar and went out into the storm. The wind tossed his hair wildly and tugged at his coat, and he was drenched through before he had gone halfway around the house. He pressed on and circled twice, looking about him in the darkness and reflecting grimly that it was no wonder his aunts had moved to the little house. It was a considerable walk to get all the way around this pile.

He made his way to the back door for the second time, and had started to go in when he changed his mind. Better go over and check on the aunts, see whether anything was wrong. Those awful fights they had. He'd taken the bullet from Violet's gun, but still—

He plodded across almost half a mile of lawn and field to the little white house, and as he approached he saw that it was lighted from top to bottom. Looked as though they were shooting tonight, all right, unless the storm had made them nervous, and they were sitting up keeping an eye on it.

He went up the few steps to the tiny back porch, but found that the door was locked. He rattled the knob and pounded on the panels, but there was no response, and he swore under his breath. The shoddy little door was loose on its hinges, and if he had a screwdriver, he could open it in two minutes. He went down the steps again and splashed through mud and water around to the front.

The door was open here, and he began to run. He found that it was not swinging, but had jammed against the floor. He gave it a wrench and it scraped free and flew shut with a loud bang. He swung around and went into the parlor holding his breath, but it was empty and peaceful. There was no one in the dining room, and it was neat and in order save for two plates and two glasses set out on the round, lace-covered table. There were cookies on the plates, but there was no sherry. The glasses were filled with milk.

Richard hunched his wet shoulders and glanced uneasily back into the parlor. Something was not as usual there, disarranged, but he could not decide what it was. Well, let it go. He'd better have a look around upstairs.

The two bedrooms and the bathroom were neat, and empty. He was really alarmed now, and he returned to the kitchen wondering a little wildly whether they had both gone insane and were wailing and gibbering in the storm outside the big house. He'd have to do something, go back and look again. He'd left the back door open over there. They'd be able to get in, perhaps go upstairs and frighten Ada.

He ran nearly the whole way back to the big house. He circled it again, but heard no more wailing, and found nothing. He went in and hurried upstairs and to Ada's door, where he listened carefully. There was no sound from inside, and he tiptoed away and decided to search through the other bedrooms.

It was more of a job than he had supposed. He had to fumble for light switches, and often, when he found them, there was no light anyway. Many of the rooms opened into each other. Some were connected by a bathroom, and at last he found himself in what seemed to be a sewing room, which did not open into the hall at all. He was lost by now, but he had an idea that he had worked himself toward the front of the house. He'd go on to the next room, where presumably he'd be able to get back to the hall.

He went through and found the light switch without trouble this time, but he was startled into a leap and an exclamation when he saw that someone was lying in the bed. The figure turned over, sat up, and screamed, and he saw that it was Ada.

"It's all right," he stammered, "don't be frightened. I've been searching the rooms, and I blundered in here by mistake."

She pushed the tumbled hair back from her forehead. "But what is it? You look so awful. You're all wet, and your hair hanging down. What happened to you?"

Richard peered into a mirror and tried to smooth his wet hair. He shook himself and muttered, "Too bad. My Sunday suit."

Ada pulled the sheet around her neck and stared at him. "Have you been outside, or did you take a shower with your clothes on? What *is* the matter?"

"It's the aunts. They've disappeared, and I can't find them anywhere."

"But I don't understand. Aren't they home? Who told you?"

"I've been over there. There isn't a soul in the house, and their supper is sitting on the table."

Ada's eyes had lost the dark look of sleep, and there was a puzzled frown on her forehead. "What took you over there at this time of night?"

"It was after I thought I'd heard you call. I heard the same sound again, like someone wailing outside."

"You were overtired, and imagined it," Ada said sensibly.

"I'd say so, except that the aunts are not in their house. I'm nearly sure that I heard them calling outside here. Perhaps they were frightened and came running over and then couldn't get in. I left the back door open when I went out, and I'm hoping that they got in and are somewhere in the house. I've been searching for them, which is how

I came to blunder in here. You go on back to sleep, and I'll try not to disturb you again."

Ada shook her head. "I'm wide awake now. I'll help you look for them."

"Well, that's nice of you," he said, looking pleased. "I'll wait in the hall till you get something on."

He went out, and Ada appeared presently wearing a negligee of white lace over blue chiffon, with slippers to match. He stared, and she said petulantly, "Oh, I know I'm overdressed, but this is the only robe I have left. I got it from a friend who owed me money."

"I think that spoils it a little," Richard said. "You look so glamorous, and then you tell me that the outfit is merely payment on a debt."

"I look far better in tailored things," Ada said shortly. "Come on, let's look for the aunts. We'll finish up here first."

They wandered around on the second floor for some time, but they could never feel that their search was really thorough. They both had the impression that they had done some of the rooms twice, and others not at all.

"It's such an absurd arrangement," Ada declared crossly. "All these rooms, like a maze. If I owned this place, I'd make some vast changes."

"I don't agree with you." Richard brushed at his damp trousers and left smudges of dirt. "It's interesting this way. If you fix it so that you know where you are, you'll lose the charm."

"I could do without the charm. I keep feeling that someone is dodging along ahead of us, and that we'll never be able to corner him. Why do the rooms have to open into each other, anyway? There's no privacy."

"Suppose we look around downstairs?" Richard suggested. "They may not have come up here."

"They should have heard the noise we've been making. Why don't they call out and let us know where they are?"

"I haven't been able to follow their mental processes for some time," Richard assured her. "I'm going to search downstairs, and then I'll phone the chief."

"You mean the chief of police, Oliver O'Brien?"

He nodded, and they went on downstairs together. The task was easier there, since the rooms were larger and fewer, and they were soon convinced that the aunts were nowhere about.

"Phone Miss Dedingham," Ada said. "They might have gone over there. I'll put on some coffee."

When he returned to the kitchen she was still washing out the coffeepot. "Annie's a slop," she muttered. "All the grounds left in the pot. Well, are they at Miss Dedingham's?"

"I don't know. The line must be down—I can't raise the operator. We'll have some coffee, and then I'll walk over there."

Ada put on the coffee and dropped bread into the toaster, and Richard wandered around, looking idly over the various shelves with their old-fashioned glass doors. He looked twice at some bundles wrapped in newspaper, before his brain alerted, and then he stepped over and lifted them down from the shelf.

They were the same bundles that he had last seen in the excavation at the little house.

14

Ada said, "what's this?" and picked up one of the wineglasses that Richard had unwrapped. She added, "Why, it's lovely! Who put all that newspaper around it? Maybe the aunts want to keep these things for themselves, and haven't had time to take them to the little house yet."

Richard loosened the damp collar from his neck with an uneasy finger. The person who was stealing these things for sale at an antique shop had brought them this far, after leaving them in the cellar of the little house to see whether their disappearance was noticed. He could not help suspecting Annie, and it was possible that she had used the excavation as a hiding place, without having had anything to do with digging it.

He said, "I'll unwrap these, and put them back on the shelf. They shouldn't be lying around disguised in a lot of newspaper. Someone might throw them away."

Ada nodded. "If the aunts ask for them, I'll pack them up again.

Look, why don't you try the phone? The line might have been repaired by now."

Richard went to the hall, but was unable to get any response from the phone. He considered for a moment, obscurely oppressed by the shelves of books that rose to the ceiling on the four walls. Well, he'd have to go to town and pick up Chief O.O.. The aunts must be found, and it couldn't wait. He'd stop at Miss Dedingham's first, since it was on the way.

He found that the wind had died down when he got outside again, but it was raining steadily. He took the car this time, and headed for Miss Dedingham's house. It was some distance by road, but no farther away than the little house by foot across the field.

He was relieved to see a light in what he knew to be Miss Dedingham's bedroom, and after he had parked the car he hurried up to the front door and knocked sharply. He felt sure now that the aunts were here. They had been frightened by something, and had run to their friend for help.

Doc Paunders opened the door, and he and Richard stared at each other in surprise. Doc said, "Well! Surely am glad to see you. I need some help here, boy. Miss Dedingham has had a stroke."

"Oh, I—I'm sorry." Richard stepped in, and Doc closed the door. "Are my aunts here?"

"Your aunts?" Doc shook his head. "Haven't seen them. Hernand came in a while back, with me."

Mr. Hernand was standing at the door to Miss Dedingham's bedroom, and he turned to Richard with an expression which he usually reserved for funerals. "She's done for."

Doc said, "Shh! Don't say that. Matter of fact, it's my guess she'll pull out of it."

"When did it happen?" Richard asked.

"Not so long ago. She phoned me, said she was feeling bad, and I had an idea I'd better get over here in a hurry. I know Hernand reads late at night, and it occurred to me to pick him up on the way. Good thing, too. I've needed him. but we'll have to have a nurse now. She can't be left alone. What are you wandering around at this time of night for, anyway?"

"My aunts are missing. I thought I heard them calling outside, but I haven't been able to find them, and they're not at the little house.

Are you sure Miss Dedingham didn't phone them and ask them to come to her, since she was ill?"

"She may have." Doc shrugged. "But certainly I haven't laid eyes on them since I got here."

"They are not at home?" Mr. Hernand asked.

"There was no one in the house, and the front door was wide open."

"Trouble," Mr. Hernand said, washing his hands together. "We must find them. Something has happened."

"Suppose we search this old barn first," Doc suggested. "You never know about those two."

"Why would they hide here?" Mr. Hernand wondered.

Richard felt that he could not spend the time looking through another old mansion, and he said quickly, "You two search the place, will you? Outside, as well. I'm going into town to get O.O. It's his business now. I'll bring out a nurse, if I can find one, or at least someone who can look after Miss Dedingham for the time being."

They looked at him for a moment, and then Mr. Hernand nodded, but Doc said restlessly, "I have to get home. I can't—"

"You'll have to stay. I can't be left here alone," Mr. Hernand cried, his eyes showing panic. "Suppose she came out of it. I wouldn't know what to do."

"She'll be like that for some time," Doc said irritably. "I'll be back by that time, anyway."

Richard said, "Doc, you'll have to stay here. You can't leave Hernand alone with Miss Dedingham, and anyway, I'm counting on you to search for my aunts. I won't be long, and I promise to bring back someone who can take over."

Doc Paunders scowled, but in a resigned sort of way, and Richard left the two of them climbing the stairs to the second floor. He hurried to his car, calling his aunts by name once or twice on the way, but the storm seemed to throw his voice back into his throat.

It was four o'clock when he at last roused Chief of Police Oliver O'Brien. The chief was a conscientious man, and he rose immediately without profane comment. He was dressed in a remarkably short time, and backed his car out of its garage.

"I'll have to try and find a nurse to take out to Miss Dedingham," Richard said. "She's ill. But I'll follow you as soon as I can."

"You're gonna have trouble," the chief warned him dourly. "People been phoning me all the time. I got to produce a nurse. I told them I'm a policeman, *not* a nurses' registry. But most of them, it just hits their ears and bounces right back on you."

"Well, I'll do what I can," Richard said. "See you later."

The chief roared away in his car, and Richard went to his mother's house. He still had his key, and he let himself in and called to her from the lower hall. She appeared after a while, struggling into a robe and blinking in the light. "What are you doing here?" she demanded crossly. "You scared me half to death."

"Well—"

"Left your wife already?"

"Of course not. It's the aunts. They've disappeared."

Mrs. Balron laughed. "I always suspected that they flew around at night, sucking the blood of young people."

"Mother, please! It's serious."

She gave him a cold eye. "Did you wake me from a good, sound sleep to tell me that those two old bats are missing?"

"No, not just that. Miss Dedingham has had a stroke, and it seems to be next to impossible to get a nurse. Doc Paunders and Hernand are with her now, and they can't leave until someone turns up to look after her. I thought perhaps you'd be willing to help out."

"Oh. Did you? At my age I'm supposed to take up nursing?"

Richard sighed. "I just want you to go over there for a while so that those two old men can get some rest. You can sit at the phone, then, until you dig up a nurse. The chief says there's not one to be had, but I somehow think *you* could get one."

"Scoop up the soft soap and put it away," said Mrs. Balron, still chilly. "I could sit down here at my own phone until I dig up a nurse."

"All right, any way you like. I'll leave it in your lap. Good night, dear."

He dropped a kiss on her forehead, and she backed away from him. "Oh, sure! Any work or trouble of any kind is always left in some poor, wretched woman's lap! Doc and Hernand got caught up there, and so of course they're squealing for some woman to come and take over. If it wasn't for the fact that Miss Dedingham is a woman, I'd let them squeal 'til their tonsils dropped off, except that they wouldn't. They'd just walk off, after a while, and leave Miss Dedingham to the care of her horses, which would be better care than she's getting from them. All right. Go on, beat it! Do your man's noble work and leave the slops for me. I'm a woman, unfortunately."

Richard departed in a hurry before she could change her mind. He headed for the little house, and the yellow convertible passed him on the way. He shook his head and hoped that she'd make it safely, and decided that he'd have to speak to her again about her wild driving.

The door was open at his aunts' house, and the chief's car was parked at the curb. Richard pulled up behind and hurried in.

"That you?" the chief called from the parlor. "You got married here this afternoon, huh?"

"Yes. Brilliant affair."

"Sure. Whoever cleaned up afterwards, it was some messy job. Look." He swept a flashlight around the floor. "The mice are gonna have a swell time, they leave it like this."

Richard nodded. "That's Annie. She doesn't expect you to look at the floor with a flashlight. And my aunts never soil their hands with housework."

"Is that so?" said the chief distantly.

Richard glanced at him and realized, tardily, that he had been offensive. His own aunts were above housework, and Annie was O.O.'s cousin. He cleared his throat and tried to make amends. "I'd never bring up my daughters as my aunts were brought up. Everyone should learn how to take care of himself in all ways."

The chief said, "Yeah," and added irrelevantly, "My grandfather in the old country was a baronet."

"That so?" murmured Richard, who had heard it before. "Have you looked upstairs?"

"Sure have. Nobody there, *or* in the cellar."

"You looked in the cellar?"

"Sure did. I hadda pick the lock. Pete helped me."

"Where's Pete?"

"He's looking out back."

Richard sent an uneasy glance around the walls of the parlor. But there wouldn't be anything. He had removed the bullet from the gun. His straying eyes suddenly became fixed, and he took a quick step forward. It was there, embedded neatly in the wall—a bullet.

15

Richard walked over to the wall and examined the bullet. It was embedded in the woodwork at the archway to the hall, and he fingered it tentatively. How could they have shot at each other tonight? Why would they? There'd been an argument, of course, and something said about "six times." It had been futile for him to have removed the bullet from the gun. Chances were they always examined them before shooting. But this one in the woodwork had missed. Were there any others? He began to prowl around the walls.

"You sure got itchy feet, son," the chief observed. "Don't you like that there wallpaper, or what?"

"You're some sleuth, you are," Richard said, returning to the woodwork. "What do you call this?"

"Huh?" The chief walked over and pulled his glasses from an inside pocket. He stared long at the embedded bullet, and then walked into the dining room and drank one of the glasses of milk at one gulp. He wiped his mouth carefully with his sleeve, and then absently brushed off the sleeve.

"What do you make of it?" Richard asked.

"It's serious, my boy, no doubt about that. Looks like homicide."

"You think so?"

"Certainly I think so. Didn't anybody throw that bullet. It was shot from a gun."

"I'm inclined to agree with you," Richard said gravely. "It would take a strong man to throw a bullet that far into the woodwork."

The chief gave him a severe look. "This is not the time, nor neither the place, for joking. There's been a shooting here, which scared those poor old ladies out of the house. Thing is, how far did they get before this here vicious killer caught up with them? Looks bad, I'm telling you."

He went to the hall and picked up the phone, and Richard, following him, muttered, "I think you should know a few things."

"Listen, Smedley," said the chief, "I *do* know a few things. Hello, Susie? Get me the boys, all of them. Looks like there's been a killing here. Round 'em up and send 'em out. Pete's the only one here already. O.K., g'by." He replaced the phone with a firm hand.

"Why do you jump to the conclusion that there's been a killing?" Richard asked in a bothered voice. "*That* bullet didn't kill anyone."

The chief seemed newly cloaked in authority and importance. He narrowed his eyes at Richard and said, "You go on back to your bride, young man, you're only in my way here. Anything develops, I'll see you get notified."

Richard returned to his car, pondering on the downfall of the name of Balron, in one generation. The chief had addressed him, in a patronizing manner, as "young man," and yet he would hardly have dared to address the aunts at all. Also, if they had deigned to notice him, he would certainly have bowed from the waist.

He decided to stop at Miss Dedingham's and check on the situation there. He found the front door unlocked and walked in.

The two men were still there, and they were seated with Mrs. Balron at a bridge table, eating something.

"I thought Doc had to go home and get some sleep."

Doc Paunders fiddled with the handle of his coffee cup and cleared his throat, and Mr. Hernand rose uncertainly to his feet.

"We, er, we were just eating this little snack your mother made for us. We needed it badly—completely exhausted, you know."

"You want something, Richard?" Mrs. Balron asked. "Cup of coffee?"

"No, thanks. Has any of you looked for the aunts?"

"You mean they haven't showed up yet?"

"They have not. Did you men look outside?"

Doc Paunders cleared his throat again, but with more authority. "The weather outside is hardly the thing for us old-timers. We looked around inside here, of course, but were unable to find them. However, this is a large house and there are any amount of hiding places, locked doors with no keys in them, and Miss Dedingham is in no condition to supply keys or information."

Richard turned to Mrs. Balron. "Perhaps you could find the keys, Mother. Will you try while I look around outside?"

"Richard, will you for God's sake go home and go to bed!" she said in complete exasperation. "Those two will turn up in their own good time, whether you get pneumonia or not. If you'll go straight home, I'll promise to find the damned keys and search the house thoroughly as well. I've always been curious about this place, anyway, and I'll go into every nook and cranny. I will also look in on Miss Dedingham regularly, so do take that sour puss away and put it on a pillow."

"All right," Richard agreed mildly. "Have you tried to get a nurse?"

"How could I try to get a nurse when the telephone line is down?"

"I must have been the last to get a call from here," Doc Paunders said. "By the time I got here the phone was dead. I know, because I tried it."

Richard raised his wet shoulders in a shrug. "I thought it might have been repaired. The aunts' phone is working."

"Must be a different line," Mrs. Balron yawned. "Go on. Get out of here, will you?"

Richard returned to his car and started the engine, and then slid out from behind the wheel and made a cautious circle of the house. He hated to think of them wandering around in this storm, frightened and calling out for help. But there was no sound of wailing here, nor any sign of them. He could see lights in the distance, in the direction of the little house, and he realized that the chief's men were searching for them there.

He returned to the big house, and as he approached the huge garage at the rear his headlights picked up Pat leaning against the wall at the back. He ran the car in and switched off the engine, and Pat observed, "Some storm."

Richard told him about the aunts, but he seemed unconcerned.

"Them silly old wimmin always roamed around some at night. Ain't no sense fussin' about it."

"But they didn't wander around in a storm like this?"

"I wouldn't say no. They was always crazy as bedbugs. Here I gotta lose sleep gettin' up to fix some black iris so they'll bloom first thing in the mornin'."

"Did you say *they* were crazy as bedbugs?" Richard muttered.

There was a light shining from the back door, and he hurried across and went in. He found Ada standing at the door to the butler's pantry, her eyes enormous in her white face. He stopped abruptly and said, "I scared you. I'm sorry. Why didn't you go back to bed?"

She drew a long breath and moved away from the door. "It's all right. I've been between here and the dining room all the time—too sissy even to go upstairs again. This house is awful enough, but when you add wailing voices outside—"

"You heard them too?" he asked quickly.

"Well, no, I don't think so. Probably just the wind. Did you find the aunts?"

Richard shook his head. "The chief and all the town cops are out searching. But you'd better go to bed. I'm sorry you were frightened. I'll take you up to your room."

"I'd rather wait till it's light." She shivered and hugged herself with her arms. "I don't see how I can sleep when the aunts are in trouble of some sort. Where *can* they be?"

"It will be light soon," Richard said. "If the chief brings any word, I'll wake you up. Lock your door, and you'll be all right."

"Look under the bed and in the closet first," Ada sighed. "All right. You escort me up, and please don't leave the house again until morning. I'll pack up and get out then."

He took her arm as they went out into the hall. "Don't say that. The only place we could go is to my mother's house. I don't believe you'd like to live with your mother-in-law."

Ada gave a hysterical little giggle. "I never thought of Mrs. Balron as my mother-in-law. She doesn't look like one."

"You'd find out," Richard said ominously. "You'd have no say whatever in the house, as I never had any say. You'd have to do as you were told. It's better here. You are the mistress of a fine mansion, with someone to do the dishes at night."

"To be sure. I have only about two dozen rooms to clean, and it's going to be pretty tiring, since I can't get any sleep at night. I'll be too scared."

Richard went into her bedroom with her and examined the windows and the door to the other room, and then looked in the closets and under the bed. There was another door to a back hall which he fastened carefully before leaving by the door to the main hall.

"I'll wait until I hear you lock this door," he told her, "and I'll leave my door open so that I can hear you if you call."

He listened until she turned the key, and then he went across to his own room. He pulled out a cigarette and flung himself down on the bed in his damp clothes, too tired for the moment even to remove them. He watched the smoke from his cigarette drifting toward the ceiling, and began to think about the bullet that had been embedded in the woodwork. So they'd been playing Russian roulette again, and that one had missed. The "six times" meant that they would play six times, and then settle on something if they were both living. Now, who was pinching their stuff? Would Annie know enough to pinch the right things? Those had been very special pieces that had been in that new grave in the cellar of the little house. The new grave— He got up off the bed quickly. Those packages he'd found downstairs— They'd been removed to make room for a body newly dead.

16

He left the light burning in his room and crept out to the hall and down the stairs. He went out by the back door and swore steadily for some time because he had forgotten to provide himself with some sort of a raincoat, and it was still raining. But he would not go back.

He looked toward the little house as he hurried across the lawn, and saw that the flashlights had disappeared. They'd given up, then. But they shouldn't give up. They'd *have* to find those two old ladies.

He went in the back door of the little house and somewhat startled the chief and three of his men, who were playing a comfortable game of poker. The chief saw the look on Richard's face and decided instantly that his only defense was a sharp attack.

"Where you been, fella? We looked all over for you. We got nothing to go on here, but we got to stay in case they turn up. Don't think we're having fun, neither. They'll be mad as hell when they find us in their kitchen. But that's a cop's life, all dooty and no reward."

Richard set his jaw and took the key from the back door. He went to the door of the cellar, and then discovered that the chief had not bothered to lock it again. He glanced over his shoulder. "You'd better come down with me, O.O. I have a hunch about this."

They descended together, and Richard pointed out the cut linoleum in the corner. He said flatly, "I'm surprised that you didn't discover this yourself."

The chief was chagrined. He muttered, "I had my glasses off. That dimwit was with me should of caught it, he has young eyes. Anyways, if you knew about it, why didn't you tell me earlier?"

Richard dropped to his knees without answering. Why hadn't he told the chief? But he'd thought it was only a hiding place for the stolen articles.

He pulled irritably at the linoleum, but it seemed to be stuck. The chief played a flashlight, and Richard saw, then, that it had been nailed. He mopped vaguely at perspiration trickling down his neck and supposed that he'd have to get some tools. No, wait, it could be nailed only to the board underneath, and the board was loose. Below that, there was only earth.

The chief puffed to a kneeling position beside him, and together they pried up the board to which the linoleum was nailed.

She was covered only lightly with earth. Apparently there hadn't been time to bury her properly, but she was draped from head to foot in a bloodstained shawl.

The chief gave a queer little grunt, stretched a tentative arm, and then withdrew it. Neither of them wanted to uncover her, and they remained still in a silence that presently became too much for the chief. He scrambled to his feet and lurched to the foot of the stairs, where he bawled, "Pete!"

Richard took the shawl off. He had to make sure that it was Miss Ivy, but he was unprepared for the horror that lay under it. He drew back with a sharp, unintelligible exclamation, and the chief came blundering back.

It looked as though she had been killed with a hatchet. There were great bloody gashes on her face and arms and body. Richard turned away, and the chief caught at his arm.

"Which one is it?"

"Aunt Ivy."

"Are you sure?"

"Yes, I'm sure."

It *was* Aunt Ivy. And Aunt Violet was still running around loose, perhaps with the hatchet clutched in her bloody little hand. She'd missed her shot, and she must have gone berserk suddenly, finished

Ivy off, and then dragged her down to the cellar. No, she was too frail for that. Perhaps poor Ivy had fled to the cellar and Violet had followed and attacked her, and then pushed her into the grave. It would be easy enough. She could have done that.

Pete had come down, but his stomach was unequal to the occasion and he had retired to rest on the floor with his back sagging against the wall.

The chief was furious. "Some cop, you are. Why don't you maybe get a job as a ladies' hairdresser or a dancing teacher?" He walked to the foot of the stairs to call the other two men, but they were already on the way down.

"You fellas lift her out. We got to see if the other one is underneath."

"No." Richard said quickly.

"Why not?" the chief demanded, turning a sharp eye on him.

Richard started to say that he had heard Violet wailing around the big house, but stopped himself. How did he know that it had been Violet, after all? He shook his head and said nothing.

The two men lifted the battered body from its grave, but there was only the earth underneath it. The chief quickly threw the shawl over Miss Ivy again, and then turned to Richard.

"How did you know the other one wasn't there?"

Richard stared down at the linoleum and compressed his lips for a moment. "I didn't know, but I'd seen this hole before, and I thought it wasn't deep enough, unless it had been dug out since."

"Yeah? So when did you see this here hole before? And why did you clam up about it?"

"I didn't, really. You said you had searched the cellar, and I suppose I assumed that you had found this grave. It never occurred to me that you might have missed it."

"That so?" The chief's eyes were slitted and glittering. "And what brought you tripping over your feet in such a hurry to take a look in there now, if you thought we already looked?"

Richard rubbed his balled fist across his forehead and muttered, "Come upstairs, will you? I'll tell you all I know about it. And give me a cigarette. Mine are wet."

They were both glad to escape from the cellar, and after they had found chairs in the kitchen the chief hauled out a pack of cigarettes.

Richard told him of Annie's fears about the grave, and of the things he had found hidden there. "I really never gave any thought as to whether you'd found the hole or not," he finished. "It just struck me all of a sudden that the things had been moved to the big house, and not taken straight to a buyer."

"That don't sound unreasonable." The chief shook his head. "Likely the things was more handy over there."

"Well"—Richard drew on his cigarette—"did you get in touch with the woman at that antique shop? Find out who has been picking up their stuff?"

"How much time you think I've had?" the chief demanded in an injured voice. "I went out there, sure, but she was closed up. She lives somewheres in the city and drives out each day. Didn't any of the people around know where she lives."

"But surely you can find out?"

"Certainly I can find out. She'll open her shop in the morning and I'll find out then. I'm going out first thing." He looked at the window and saw that it was gray with dawn. "Morning now, I guess, but it's still raining."

Richard stood up and stretched, and the chief yawned, and then closed his mouth with a snap. "Right now, we got to find Miss Violet before she kills anyone else."

Richard walked quickly to the back door. "I'm going now. Call me when you want me. I'll be around."

He went out and started across the field, his mind tired and confused. He must tell Ada, and they'd have to arrange for a funeral, all the details. And he had to find Aunt Violet. It would be dreadful for her—the chief had made up his mind. But he must find her, hear what she had to say.

What she had to say? He'd been too tired to think straight. Miss Violet never moved those packages to make room for the body of her sister, because she had not put them there in the first place. And one thing was certain: even if she could have pulled Miss Ivy into the grave and covered her up, she could never have nailed the linoleum down to the board.

17

Richard turned around and plodded grimly back to the little house. He felt that he had to try and clear Miss Violet with the chief, for he was convinced, now, that although the bullet had missed she would never have killed Miss Ivy so horribly.

He caught the chief getting into his car, and he said, "Drop me at the big house, will you? I want to tell you something."

The chief slid in behind the wheel and grunted, "I thought you was mad, and didn't want to talk to me any more."

Richard got into the front seat beside him. "Well,ssomething just struck me. There was an intruder in their house the night before last, a man. They found him lying on the floor and thought he was dead, but I believe, now, that he was just playing dead. Probably didn't hear them come in, and he had no time to hide, so he dropped down on his face. He figured they'd run screaming at the sight of him, and they did. He was gone, of course, by the time I got there."

"Of course," said the chief, "because they wasn't any man there in the first place. My wife told me the whole story. Thing is, they drink too much of that there sherry."

"Have you ever," Richard asked, "seen them drinking that there sherry? It takes them somewhere around three hours to finish one glass. Besides, I found a bullet on the floor right where they said the man had been lying."

"So what?"

"So isn't it strange to find a bullet on the floor? In a ladies' parlor?"

"Some ladies' parlors, yes," said the chief. "But those two dames, you're apt to find anything on their floor. Look what they have in the cellar."

Richard was momentarily silenced, and the chief swung his car to a stop at the foot of the wide stone steps that led to the veranda of the big house. "You got to face it, fella," he said reasonably, "those two was nuts. Miss Violet will be put where the hatchets is kept locked up, and she can stick straws in her hair all day long and where she shoulda been years ago. I always thought they was a pair of loonies, and this proves it."

Richard got out of the car and closed the door. "You're entitled to your opinion, of course, but there's one thing you should do, and that's find out who has been stealing their things. Someone has been getting in and out of both their houses and making off with some valuable stuff, and this same person was in the little house some time between late the night before last and some time before we landed up here."

The chief eyed him warily. "How do you figure that?"

Richard reminded him of the packages that had been in Miss Ivy's grave and were currently in the big house. The chief yawned and told him to leave police business to the police, and to go and get some sleep.

"But the thing must be investigated. You can't overlook it."

"Who's overlooking anything? We'll find the thief."

"Thief *and* murderer," Richard said firmly. "Those packages were moved to make room for Miss Ivy. If Miss Violet had found them she'd have put them back where they belonged in the little house, because that's where they came from. They *had* to be moved, you see, put somewhere where they could still be sold. And you can take my word for it that Miss Violet doesn't need cash. Her account is loaded."

"Sure, sure." The chief yawned again. "The way I see it, the thief just happened to get that stuff out of the grave before Miss Violet needed to use it, and he just happened to find the grave, same as Annie did. I gotta go. See you later."

Richard felt a childish desire to shake his fist after the departing car. He sighed and plodded around to the back door, where he crept in and up the stairs to his room. It was six o'clock, and he decided that there was no use trying to sleep now. Might as well have a shower and get dressed in dry clothes. He gathered the pages of his work together and slipped them back in the brief case. He hadn't studied them properly, and he'd had no sleep. He could merely hope for the best.

It developed that there was no shower in the bathroom, but there was plenty of hot water and a huge bathtub. He filled it and climbed in, trying to remember when he had last had a bath instead of a shower. He found it unexpectedly relaxing, so much so that he dozed off and woke up only when the water slid over his nose and interfered with his breathing.

On the way back to his room he decided that the house looked nice by daylight, and he particularly admired the heavy, overall carpeting. He wondered how much it had cost.

He dressed quickly and crept down the stairs, anxious not to wake Ada. As he approached the kitchen he smelled coffee and bacon and supposed that Annie was getting breakfast for Pat and herself. Well, he'd be able to wheedle some, surely.

It was Ada in the kitchen, and she turned from the stove as he came in. "I heard you dressing, so I came down to get your breakfast. What about the aunts? I haven't heard from the chief or anyone else."

Richard sat down at the table and smiled at her. "You know, it's nice to come down and find someone getting breakfast for me."

Ada said, "I suppose so. I've never had the experience."

"You lived in hotels for some years, didn't you? Someone always prepares your breakfast in a hotel."

"That's all *you* know," Ada jeered. "Father and I had to learn about cutting expenses. We had a bun and clear tea made from the hot-water tap. Only that was lunch, really. We didn't get up for breakfast."

"What about Aunt Mignon?"

"Oh, I was a little girl, then, and we had a maid, supplied by your Aunt Violet."

"Am I supposed to just sit here?" Richard asked. "Or should I help you to bring things to the table, or what?"

"Just sit." She put bacon and eggs on the table, and then brought the coffeepot and sat down herself. There was a glass of orange juice at her place, and she poured herself a cup of black coffee.

Richard cast a glance at this austere breakfast and raised his eyebrows. "This is worse even than your hotel days. At least you had a bun, then."

"Oh, eat your bacon and eggs. Men can get as fat as pigs and nobody cares, but let a woman put on a few pounds and they sit down and think up new jokes about it."

"It's the first time I've noticed it," Richard said, "but you sound like my mother."

They were silent for a while, and then Ada asked, "Did you hear anything more last night? I don't know whether the phone is working yet or not."

They had finished the meal, and Richard took out cigarettes. He handed one to her and said carefully, "You'll have to brace yourself and take this on the chin. It's bad."

It was bad. She did not get hysterical, but she cried for some time. Eventually she whispered, "Aunt Ivy never cared for me as much as Aunt Violet, but she often went out of her way to be kind to me."

"Yes, I know."

He did not tell her of the chief's suspicions of Miss Violet, but she presently mopped at her wet eyes with a damp ball of handkerchief and asked, "Where is she, Aunt Violet? I must go to her, help her."

"She may be right in the house here somewhere," Richard said. "I wish you'd try to find her. She's most probably in a dazed condition from shock."

"Oh, the poor darling!" Ada stood up. "I'll find her. I'll search the place from attic to cellar."

She ran out of the room, and Richard sat there, thinking about the attic and the cellar. They had neglected both places in their search during the night.

Annie walked into the kitchen and came to a stop with her hands on her hips. "Well look at you. Ain't you the early bird, though? I see you finished my bacon."

"It was yours?"

"Yep—, nd what you et last night, that was mine too. But there ain't no need to apologize. Call it a wedding present. You'll get more good of it than some o' them cheesy ashtrays and vases your swell friends are gonna send."

"As you say."

"Yeah, well, just so you get your missus to do some marketing today."

"Oh." Richard burrowed into his pocket. "Suppose I give you some money, and you do the marketing for all of us. You won't be going to the little house today, so you can work here."

Annie clutched at her bosom and let out a moderate scream. "Something happened! I knew it. I says to myself time and *again*, something's gonna happen! They was gettin' mean and nasty, all of 'em."

"All of them? Who?"

"All of that old bunch, them swells."

"Could you be specific?"

"Huh?"

"Name them."

"Listen," said Annie. "You gotta tell me what *happened*. I gotta *know*."

Richard told her, and she listened in absolute silence, her eyes wide and unblinking. When he had finished she drew a long breath and slowly shook her head. "Godalmighty! I never woulda figgered it that way."

"How would you have figured it?"

Annie frowned down at the little pleats her restless hands were making in her apron. "I dunno. Miss Violet running around, alone. She must be scared crazy."

"What do you think happened?" Richard asked curiously.

She frowned into the distance and shook her head. "They all fought like wildcats, sure, but I never seen them sock each other."

"Who do you mean by 'all'?"

"All them old fools that used to come there, sittin' on their humps and drinkin' that lousy sherry. Hernand and Doc and the judge, and that poor old scarecrow, Miss Dedingham."

"And they fought together?"

"They fought like hell," Annie said simply. "Raised the rooft offa the place, but they always come back for more."

"Who were the troublemakers?"

Annie started to laugh, and then remembered Miss Ivy, and pulled a suitably sober expression across her features. "The whole shootin' match was troublemakers, so far as I could see. They made plenty trouble for me. All them sickening cookies, makes me gag to roll out the dough, any more."

"Did any of these people ever leave my aunts' home in a temper?"

"They practically always left in a temper," Annie said cheerfully.

"Then, after they all stomped out, the two old ladies would cuss at each other and maybe shut themselves in their rooms."

"Was one more ready to make up, after a fight, than the other?"

"Oh, yes. Miss Violet always got over it first," Annie answered without hesitation. "Where's she at now, anyways?"

Richard shook his head a little and made no reply. He had just remembered what had been disarranged in the parlor of the little house. Aunt Ivy's red plush chair and Aunt Violet's blue plush chair had exchanged places.

18

Annie repeated, "Where's she at?"

Richard was thinking about the chairs. It had been an old argument, and one of the few times that Miss Violet had clung stubbornly to having her own way. Miss Ivy had wanted her chair where the blue one was, and Miss Violet had declared, many times, that only over her dead body would her own chair be moved.

Ada came back into the kitchen. "I've looked upstairs, but I'd rather have someone with me when I go through the attic."

Annie nodded, but Richard scarcely heard her. "I'll have to go," he said, and stood up. "You'll work here, Annie. Do what you can, and get some food in. You're not supposed to touch anything at the little house until the chief says you can. Ada, if you find Aunt Violet, let me know, will you? I want to talk to her before the chief does. You remember that too, Annie. It won't do the chief any harm if I see her first. I believe she's suffering from shock, and I want to prepare her for him. I have a hunch that she's here somewhere, so if she shows up, get her to bed and call me."

"You'll be in court," Ada said.

"I expect to be back in the office by about noon. You can get me there, or leave a message with Mrs. Evans. Just tell her that I'm to phone home. Will you do that?"

They both nodded, and Richard said, "Right. Good-by," and took himself off.

"Well, waddya know about that!" Annie gave Ada a commiserating eye. "You had a spat already?"

Ada yawned. "I think I'll have another cup of coffee. No—no spat. He's upset about his aunts. He was very fond of them, you know."

"Yeah, I guess. Sure is tough, all this happening, just when you got married."

Ada lighted a cigarette and sipped at her coffee, and presently Pat came in. He divided a look of disfavor between Ada and his wife because he did not like breakfasting with strangers and was inclined to blame Annie for the presence of this one.

"Sit down and eat," Annie said without bothering to look at him. "I got your breakfast here, and I got something to tell you, so hang onto your chair."

She told him about Miss Ivy, and Ada, listening, had to fumble for her damp handkerchief again. Pat listened in silence and thought it over for a while before he asked, "You mean she didn't die natural?"

"That's what I just been tellin' you. I knew something was gonna happen, some awful thing, what with them livin' over *him* that way."

Pat stopped crunching toast to observe, "You're a silly woman. You think *he* coulda climbed outa that tomb and chased her with a hatchet?"

"I didn't say he did," Annie snapped. "But I still think it's askin' for trouble, goin' your way and drinkin' sherry over a graveyard. You can bet that *I* ain't gonna set foot in that house again."

"Oh?" Pat raised his face from his coffee cup. "What about Miss Violet? You gonna leave her there all alone?"

"She ain't there. I already told you that. Richard kinda thinks she's around here somewheres, but we ain't seen her. We gotta look, though. She might be sick, and maybe not able to call us. She ought to be flat on her back in bed this minute."

Pat drummed his fingers on the table and presently sighed. "Wouldn't I just, now?"

"Wouldn't you just what?" Annie demanded.

"I ast that Richard fella for some black tissue paper, and he give me an idea—carbon paper. Sez he'd bring some home, but I couldn't wait. Fellas like him mostly forget, anyways, so I go and buy some.

Got up before morning and wrapped them up on wires and stuck 'em in."

Annie brought a plate to the table for herself and sat down. "I suppose you know what you're talking about."

"Them black iris," Pat said irritably. "The ones Miss Ivy said gotta bloom right now."

"So you went to all that trouble and now Miss Ivy's where she can't see them. Do you want us to bust out cryin'?"

Ada looked at him in some astonishment. "Do you mean that you put paper flowers in the garden because Miss Ivy insisted on certain blooms at certain times?"

"Ahh, that's what *he* says," Annie sniffed. "It just ain't so. Miss Ivy always said he was the best gardener she ever knew, and sometimes she'd be surprised something wasn't blooming, so he's that conceited he hadda *make* it bloom, and Miss Ivy praisin' him up and tellin' him how they oughta exhibit at the flower show. Miss Violet never paid no heed to all that, but she's a great one for pickin' flowers all the time. She won't wear her glasses and never would, and more than once didn't I see her carefully puttin' a bunch of paper flowers in a bowl of water. I was like to bust my face, tryin' to keep it straight."

"You must be very skillful at making paper flowers," Ada said, looking at Pat.

Annie nodded. "Oh, sure, he's good. I keep tellin' him all the time, when he crabs around about this job, he could go in the business."

"I want the rest of my breakfast," Pat said.

Ada stood up. "Well, I suppose I'd better go and get *something* done."

She wandered out into the hall and stopped at the foot of the stairs, bothered by her thoughts. She'd done wrong, and perhaps Miss Ivy would not have been killed if she hadn't pushed the wedding through. She blinked over a fresh welling of tears, and then reminded herself sternly that there was no time for crying. Miss Violet must be found. Poor Aunt Violet, lying somewhere, dazed and helpless, or wandering around. Probably she had seen the dreadful attack on her sister. A wisp of thought that Miss Violet had been the attacker drifted into Ada's mind, but she brushed it away quickly. Absurd—quite impossible. But the poor dear must be found.

She started up the stairs, but turned and came down again almost immediately. It would be frightening to look through those dim, lonely rooms for a Miss Violet whose mind might be wandering. She'd get Annie to go with her.

She went back, but as she reached the butler's pantry she realized that there was someone else in the kitchen. She moved the swinging door cautiously until she was able to peer through the crack, and she saw that it was the chief. He was talking to Annie, and Ada stood very still and listened.

"They argued all the time," Annie was saying, "but that's nothing. They done that all their lives. I often thought how bored they'd be if they didn't have each other to argue with. They didn't have nothing to do, and you gotta do something with your time."

"Sure. But now, last night, before you left, didn't they have an argument that was extra special, even for them?"

"Who told you?"

"In my business," said the chief, expanding his chest a little, "you learn to put two and two together. Anyways, I'm asking the questions. What did they fight about?"

"How should I know? I was running water in the sink a lot of the time. But they was sure making a lot of noise, and when one of them sez she'd kill the other with pleasure I got scared."

"With pleasure? You sure she didn't say with a hatchet, or a knife, or the poker?"

"How much do you get when you put two and two together?" Annie asked derisively. "Or do you think my ears need cleaning out?"

Pat stood up. "I gotta go. I got work. All that rain."

The chief watched him go in silence, and then turned again to Annie. "Which one said she'd kill the other?"

"I don't know. They was screaming and carryin' on and I ain't sure who said what."

The chief sighed. "Well, what was the argument *about?* You must know that."

"No, I don't, neither. One of them said, 'Now, it's my turn. I've waited long enough,' and the other busted in with, 'Never, never, never!' and the other hollered, 'I say yes, and you can't stop it, and

I'd kill you with pleasure,' and then the other yells, 'You are right! Only over my dead body.' After that they said something about, 'Six times oughta fix it.' I thought it was time someone threw cold water on 'em and wrenched 'em apart, so I run all the way over here and got Richard. See?"

"I see," said the chief, and sighed again.

"So when we got back they was sittin' peaceful in the parlor, and butter wouldn't melt in their mouth. I felt like a fool."

The chief said, "Hmm. See, here's the way I figger it. Miss Violet killed Miss Ivy while of unsound mind. She had plenty of insane moments, I know."

"She did not. She wasn't no more insane than you. Not as much."

"You been with her so much," said the chief, looking offended, "that you can't see the woods for the trees. Now I'm telling you, she's got to be found before she kills someone else. She'll be put in an institution, where she shoulda been long ago."

"If I find her," said Annie ominously, "I'll tell her to run and hide. She don't belong in no loony bin, and ain't no one got any right to try and put her there."

The chief shifted on his chair and muttered, "We'll see, we'll see. But we got to find her, and I'm gonna look through the house, here."

Annie unfolded her tight lips. "We'll find her, the missus and me. We're all set to start lookin'."

It took Ada a moment to realize that the word "missus" applied to herself, and it caused an odd prickling along her scalp, but she silently applauded Annie's effort to keep the chief from searching the house.

The chief stood up and looked Annie in the eye. "No. I'm searching the place myself. I got a warrant."

Annie stared. "You got a warrant to search this house? No kiddin'! Where'd you get it?"

The chief looked over her head. "I wrote it out myself. Are you coming around and show me the way, or do I go alone?"

Annie jammed her fists on to her hips. "You got some nerve! Writing a warrant for this here house."

"We'll do the attic first, and work down. Come on, you think I got all day?"

Annie shook her head, but wiped her hands on her apron in obvious preparation for accompanying him, and Ada darted away and flew up the stairs to the second floor. If Aunt Violet were in the house, she must find her before the chief did.

She had a little trouble locating the attic stairs. They were shut away behind a door, but she found them just as Annie and the chief started up from the lower hall. She closed the door behind her, and crept silently up the stairs.

The attic was still and dim, and very dusty. There was narrow carpeting along a center hall, from which rooms opened on either side. They were fewer than the rooms on the second floor, and, for the most part, furnished rather plainly as bedrooms. There was one storage room, cluttered with trunks and miscellanea.

Ada went swiftly, not waiting to look in the closets, because Annie and the chief were too close behind her, but she was eventually trapped in one of the bedrooms by the sound of their feet directly outside. She slipped into the closet just as they entered, but she realized that the chief would certainly look in there, and she struggled to the back behind some old coats that hung on a center pole. But even that was no use, she thought, since her feet would show, and she was about to turn around and go back into the room when she saw that she was facing a door. It opened easily from the pressure of her hand, and she emerged into a small corner room. It was furnished with some tables and two small, upholstered chairs, one blue, and one red.

19

Ada stood looking at the two chairs and knew that she was frightened. Always the red and the blue meant Aunt Ivy and Aunt Violet, and why this companionable hideaway when they were bitterly at odds so much of the time?

There was a small bookcase and a table with a mirror against the wall. Delicate little tables stood by each chair, and a blue leather book lay on the table by the blue chair, and a red leather book on the table by the red chair. The gray rug was thick and soft.

She heard the chief open the door of the closet, and stood quite still while he rattled the hangers that supported the old coats, but he backed out again apparently without having seen the farther door. She drew a quick breath of relief and wondered whether Annie knew about this room.

She waited until she heard them leave, and when they had gone down to the second floor she descended cautiously. She had decided that she might as well go to the main floor and look for Aunt Violet there.

She went down and began a careful, diligent search. She went slowly and omitted nothing. She lingered in the conservatory because she liked it, and ended with a tour of the verandas, of which there were three. She surveyed the last one a little wearily and thought that she'd have it removed. Two were surely enough. Then she twisted her hands and wondered how she could have thought of anything so frivolous, with poor Aunt Ivy lying dead, and poor Aunt Violet in some awful, unknown trouble.

She went in again and met Annie and the chief at the foot of the main staircase. "She isn't down here. I've looked, but I suppose you'll want to search for yourself."

"Good morning, Mrs. Balron," said the chief, putting on his company manners. "I've almost finished here, and then I won't need to bother you any more." He pushed Annie ahead of him and made off toward the back of the house.

The sound of the knocker on the front door crashed through the hall, and Ada gave a little cry. She waited for a moment until her breathing had quieted, and then went along and slowly pulled the door open.

Mrs. Balron poured over the sill and yelled cheerfully, "Well, my *dear!* Isn't this *awful?* Do you think I ought to ride in the first funeral car as one of the chief mourners? It's been bothering me ever since I heard. My girlfriends take these things so seriously."

"Come on to the kitchen," Ada said, "we'll have some coffee. How did you hear about it?"

"Well, I phoned a friend of mine this morning when they got the wires fixed. I had to do something. The men had left, of course, since a woman, myself, had turned up to look after Miss Dedingham. And she, poor soul, out to the wide—I thought she was going to die any minute. I think they ought to get the young doctor for her, but who am I, except a vulgar outsider?"

Ada had not heard about Miss Dedingham, and Mrs. Balron had to explain. Ada shook her head a little. "You can't tell me that her stroke wasn't brought on by something that happened last night. She must have seen something. Perhaps she saw Aunt Violet. Oh, I *wish* we could find her!"

Mrs. Balron gave Ada a searching look. "Yes, I suppose you're grieved. Cry if you want to. I'm frank to say that it means nothing to me, and I'm no hypocrite. Anyway, stop worrying. Violet will turn up. She always has. Listen to the gossip I got over the phone this morning."

"Who's with Miss Dedingham now?" Ada asked.

"One of my girlfriends. I'm supposed to be getting some sleep, but I have another friend trying to get a nurse, and I simply had to see you. You and Richard getting married like that, it's all over town that you paid him a million dollars to do it so that you could cover up your real love interest, some woman's husband—"

Ada started up from her chair with her eyes flashing, and Mrs. Balron went on composedly, "Sit down and don't act so surprised. You know darned well it was *some* sort of an arrangement, and so do I. But we'll have to issue a statement."

Ada relaxed into her chair again and said, "Statement be damned! They can think and say what they like. I only wish I had a million dollars. You can rest assured I wouldn't pay it to anyone for any-thing."

"Naturally not," Mrs. Balron agreed. "But he went in yesterday and bought that car, which was partly my fault, and of course every-one thinks he's started to spend the million."

"Oh, yes, the car." Ada cleared her throat. "That little blue job would be far more suitable for you. It really doesn't go with this house. You'd better have it, and we'll take the yellow."

"Nothing doing," said Mrs. Balron amiably. "In a way, that blue car is a sort of wedding present from me. I sent him out to buy it for you, so don't shove it back in my face."

"Oh." Ada cleared her throat again. "I didn't mean— I merely thought you might like the blue sedan better."

"No."

"Oh."

"Why *did* you marry Richard all of a sudden like that?" Mrs. Balron asked curiously.

"You want a statement from me?"

"Sure."

Ada stood up. She wore the lace robe, and she pulled it tightly around her slim waist. "I have always loved Richard. I can remember the first time I saw him—"

"When was that?"

"The way his hair curled around his temples … I can remember—"

"Richard," said Mrs. Balron, "never had a curl on his head from the day he was born."

"You're only his mother. You can't know how I feel. His damp hair curling around his hot little temples, and you never even saw it."

Mrs. Balron adjusted her spring hat with a firm hand. "Does all this drool mean that you're going to stand pat on the fact that it was a marriage for love?"

"Yes."

"Well, you're not fooling me, and drool or no drool, I don't think you're going to fool anyone else. But have it your own way."

Ada offered her a cigarette, and she puffed for a while in silence. "So you love him, and you tricked him into a marriage," she observed presently.

"I did no such thing!" Ada declared indignantly.

"Yes, you did. I know he got into one of his silly tempers, and I don't really blame you for taking advantage of the situation, but you have to remember that the whole town knows it was you who got around Judge Meeklyn to let you get married the same day you got the license. And by the way, how did you work that? Did you give him five dollars?"

"Don't be silly. I merely said I had to leave town tomorrow and I wanted to marry my beloved first, so he said he'd fix it."

"I guess you flapped your eyes and hips around at him. The judge always was a sucker for a pretty girl, even though he spent his life hanging around the Balron pair and Miss Dedingham."

"Didn't he ever marry?"

"Oh, yes, but his wife packed up and left after a dozen years of him. She took the children and went back to live with her father, who was a widower."

"Is he divorced?"

"No, she died. The children come and see him sometimes."

"And so he hung around Aunt Ivy and Aunt Violet," Ada said thoughtfully. "Didn't they have other beaux? They must have, only they never would discuss it with me."

Mrs. Balron laughed heartily. "They didn't have anything to discuss, at least Miss Ivy didn't. At that, I guess Miss Violet could have had her pick of Doc Paunders, Hernand, and the judge, only first her father wouldn't let her marry, and after he died Miss Ivy wouldn't have it. Poor old Ivy never had a beau to my knowledge. If she did, I'd be most surprised."

Annie spoke up from the butler's pantry. "I'm glad that dumb goat, O.O., didn't find the little attic room them two old maids used to go to. All the time they spent there, and I never seen it once. I woulda snooped, only they kept it locked all the time."

20

Annie pushed through the swinging door from the Butler's pantry, and Mrs. Balron said, "What little room?"

"It's a sort of little secret room offa one of the closets, up there. If I told O.O. about it, he woulda had me huntin' high and low for the key."

"You wouldn't have had to look for the key," Ada said. "The door's open. I think Aunt Violet must have been there and left it that way."

"No, sir!" Annie shook her head. "She'd never leave that door unlocked in her right mind. I know, I tried it often enough." She squinted thoughtfully and added, "I'm goin' up now. I always wanted to see that room."

"It's not worth the climb," Ada assured her. "There's nothing to see. Two chairs, some tables."

"Yeah, well— But seems I oughta look at it anyways, after I been locked out for so long."

"Where did Aunt Violet meet her beaux before her father died?" Ada asked. "In the garden, maybe?"

Annie shook her head again, and Mrs. Balron said, "No. They'd invite her out, and she'd meet them in restaurants—afternoon tea, and that sort of thing. More than once her father came around and dragged her home, and took time out to be very rude to the man who was with her at the time."

"But then, why didn't she get married after he died?"

"Miss Ivy wouldn't have it, although I don't know how she stopped her. Maybe Annie does."

Annie sniffed. "She was scared to get married, if you ask me."

"Well"—Mrs. Balron shrugged—"those men were after her money, anyway."

Annie nodded in agreement. "Sure, that's all."

"But the men are all in comfortable circumstances," Ada said.

Mrs. Balron pursed her lips. "That doesn't mean a thing. Men are never satisfied, when it comes to money. They want all they can lay their hands on. Look at Richard. He makes enough, but everyone is ready to believe that he got married for money yesterday."

"How's that?" Annie asked.

"You haven't been around to hear the gossip, yet."

"Annie could *get* around," Ada suggested, "and spread the right word."

"Yes." Mrs. Balron looked straight at Annie. "They married for love alone."

"Yeah," said Annie, "me too, and a lot of other dames. But you sure forget that angle when you've cleaned up after 'em for a few years."

"It was my fault that we married in such a hurry," Ada said firmly. "I rushed the thing, and I shouldn't have. I realize now, that a suitable interval—"

"Look, I have to take off," Mrs. Balron interrupted. "I have things to do. Would you like a lift in to town, Ada, to do anything? I see the car is gone. He always runs off with it if you don't keep an eye on him."

"I've been searching for Aunt Violet," Ada explained. "I think I'd better stay here and go on with it. I *must* find her."

Annie rooted in her pocket and pulled out some bills. "You better do some marketing, miss. Here's the money Richard give me. He told me to get some things, but I ain't got the time. I'm supposed to clean this great barn of a place, and how many hours does he think there is in a day, anyways? Some nerve. But I ain't goin' back to that little white house no more."

Ada stood up. "Perhaps I'd better go with you if we need food. Write out a list, will you, Annie? I'll throw on a few clothes, if you'll wait for me, Mrs. Balron."

"All right. Only, hurry."

Ada returned looking slim and smart in a tweed suit, and Annie handed over a list with the remark that if they didn't have veal, to get pork.

Ada nodded absently and asked, "Did the chief look in the cellar when he was searching for Miss Violet?"

"Sure did, and me keepin' an eye peeled to see he didn't sneak none of that likker down there."

"And there was no trace of her? No sign?"

"Nope. Are you comin' back for lunch?"

"No," said Mrs. Balron. "I shall take her out to lunch."

"Good."

Ada was bothered by doubts as to whether she should be abandoning, even temporarily, the search for Aunt Violet. Surely the poor dear could not have wandered far, and she ought to stay and find her.

She expressed some of this to Mrs. Balron, who hooted impatiently. "You've looked under all the carpets for her already, haven't you? What more are you supposed to do? If she's in the house, she's been running away from you from room to room, and she can't be very sick if she can dodge like that. She'll turn up when it suits her, all in one piece and asking for a glass of sherry."

"I wouldn't worry so much if I weren't afraid that she's a bit out of her mind."

"She's been out of what little mind she has for years," Mrs. Balron said comfortably. "Let her run the chief around by the nose. It's his job, and he needs the exercise. Your job is to get food into the house, even though the master has taken the only available vehicle into town. The poor, miserable woman is always supposed to produce the food, trudge for it, stagger home under the weight of it, but *get* it. All the really boring jobs are hers."

"You shouldn't try to stir up trouble between a bride and groom while they are still on their honeymoon," Ada said, laughing.

Mrs. Balron drove straight to the hotel. "We'll eat in the restaurant here. It's only eleven-thirty, but I haven't had breakfast yet. Miss Dedingham had nothing in the larder, and you didn't offer me anything but coffee."

"Don't," said Ada, "put on that act for me. I'm no mind reader, and you could have asked."

In the restaurant they were informed by a black-coated waiter that he and his brothers would not start serving lunch until noon. He suggested that they go into the lounge and have a cocktail while they waited.

Ada agreed that that would do very well and headed for the cocktail lounge with Mrs. Balron trailing and protesting. "It's all right for you, but I haven't had breakfast. We could go to the drugstore."

"Hush," said Ada in a low voice, "there's the chief talking to Judge Meeklyn. Maybe we can find out if there's anything new about Miss Violet. I don't want him to find her, and if he has, I want to know about it."

They sat down at an adjacent table, but Judge Meeklyn and the chief did not seem to notice them. The two men were talking in low, earnest tones, and Ada was unable to catch so much as a word. She settled back into her chair with a sigh.

Suddenly Judge Meeklyn's face reddened. He banged the table with his fist and raised his voice. "She's *got* to be there!"

The chief's murmur was conciliatory, and Mrs. Balron leaned so far out of her chair in an effort to hear that she nearly overbalanced. But the men were talking quietly again. It was impossible to hear anything, and Mrs. Balron was unable to stand the strain. She got up and walked over to their table.

"Good morning, Judge. Morning, Chief. Now, don't get up. I just wanted to say hello. But do tell me—did you ever find out who stole the Misses Balron's beautiful tea set?"

Judge Meeklyn was on his feet, but the chief looked up gloomily from his chair.

"Miss Ivy sold that there tea set herself."

21

From her own table Ada said clearly, "That's an absolute lie. Aunt Ivy did no such thing."

The lounge was too dimly lighted for the chief's expression to be manifest, but he made some sort of a noise. Before he could become articulate a voice spoke up behind them.

"Hello," Richard said. "What is it? A conference? You must have found Miss Violet since you're all sitting here comfortably drinking. How is she?"

"We have not found Miss Balron," said the chief austerely. "Not for want of looking, neither. What I think, you people are hiding her, and I'm writing out a warrant for her arrest, see? That way, you got to hand her over or I'll paste one on you for aiding and abetting a criminal to escape."

"What is the charge?" Richard demanded.

"Murder."

Ada tapped nervously at the base of her cocktail glass and said, "I think you're being absurd. You'll have everyone laughing at you."

"What's the evidence?" Richard asked.

The chief stood up and roared, "Never mind about the evidence. I got plenty! You better produce her, that's all."

"Now, wait a minute, Chief," Richard said quietly. "Why don't you make out your warrant to read 'material witness'? Be a lot safer for you."

"Pardon me," said the chief, "but I'm busy. It was just a friendly warning in case you're hiding her."

"We're *not* hiding her," Ada protested. "I've looked and looked, everywhere."

"Yeah." The chief nodded. "Running around ahead of me, trying to find her first. I saw you. But I don't know if you did or not."

"I did *not*."

The chief departed, wearing his bulldog expression, and Judge Meeklyn chuckled. "He is a little disturbed, and somewhat distrustful."

Richard turned to his mother and said crossly, "What are you doing in here today? It doesn't look well. You too, Ada—why couldn't you both have stayed at home?"

Mrs. Balron ignored him and rolled her eyes at Ada. "You see how it is? I'm dragged out of my bed in the middle of the night to nurse the sick friend of *three* men, while *they* retire to their beds and snore on their fat backs. So when I finally get relief and creep off to restore myself with a little breakfast I'm reproved and told that I should be at home. Doing my housework, I suppose, in my fatigued state."

"Shh," Richard whispered uneasily. "Your breakfast is all right, but why the cocktail lounge?"

"You're here, aren't you? And you're closer to the people involved in the tragedy than I am."

"Shh. Yes, I know, but I've had a hard morning in court. I really need a drink."

"Oh, sure," said Mrs. Balron, "of course. Would you like me to stroke your brow? I've only been changing Miss Dedingham's bed, with her in it, and washing her body. You need a drink if you carry home a bag of groceries, but I have been merely lifting and dragging Miss Dedingham's—believe me—heavy body. Waiter, bring me a double martini."

"All right, all right," Richard muttered. "Sorry. Waiter, not a double martini. My mother couldn't hold it, she's only trying to show off. Bring her a single weak Manhattan."

"Does that bring the fight to a close?" Judge Meeklyn inquired mildly.

Ada said, "I don't know why the chief thinks Miss Ivy sold her own tea set."

The judge started to answer, but Mrs. Balron had not yet finished with her son. She said, "Furthermore, you expect your wife to trudge two full miles to town in order to buy food for you. I am kind enough to give her a lift, and she accompanies me in here because I need a drink, so you snarl at her too."

Richard glanced at Ada and sighed. "She already has her drink, so it's quite evident that *you* accompanied *her* in here. I don't believe you even thought of ordering a drink until you lost your temper."

"Oh, shut up!" said Mrs. Balron. "The dining room isn't open yet."

"Richard," Ada persisted, "the chief said that Miss Ivy sold her own Royal tea set."

Richard looked up sharply, and Judge Meeklyn cleared his throat. "It seems to be true. I went out there with him this morning, and the woman gave a very convincing description of Miss Ivy."

"What was the description?" Richard asked.

"Oh, elderly woman with gray hair, forbidding expression—that sort of thing."

"That could describe thousands of women."

"Yes, yes, certainly, but she was wearing that cameo pin and came in the electric. I feel that that is conclusive."

"Yes"—Richard frowned down at the table—"but I can't understand it. She had no need whatever to sell her stuff. There was plenty of money, and no one to question her use of it."

Judge Meeklyn raised his massive shoulders and let them drop again, and Ada moved restlessly in her chair.

"We could go in and have lunch now."

Mrs. Balron got up immediately. "Coming, Richard?"

"Not yet. I'll have to finish your drink so that it won't be wasted."

She clacked away on her high heels. "Come on, Ada. Leave the men to their loafing and tippling. They can afford the time, but we're women and have things to do."

Richard grinned a farewell, but it faded rapidly from his face. He was unsure as to how the morning's proceedings had gone. He was tired, and he had to get out and question that woman at the antique shop himself. He felt a bit light-headed.

Judge Meeklyn was talking in a low, serious voice. "You see, it was the blows that killed her. There's no bullet wound. Very strange case. Very strange, indeed. The bullet in the wall— I wonder, now. Perhaps she tried to shoot Miss Violet and missed, and Miss Violet lost her head and took the poker to her and killed her—"

"Then who the devil dug that grave in the cellar?"

"Well"—the judge coughed and drummed his fingers on the

table—"I wouldn't worry too much about that. Chances are they did it themselves. Perhaps they were merely preparing to be laid to rest beside their father. You know that they were a bit morbid."

Richard supposed that it was possible, but he was far from satisfied. He got up and went to a booth where he phoned Annie and asked whether she had found Miss Violet.

"No," Annie told him, "I been cleaning here, but I ain't seen her. But seems like she must be around. Pat had four of them black iris this morning, and now they're all gone. You know how she used to like pickin' black iris."

Richard hung up and pressed the tips of his fingers against his temples. He ought to get out there. He was bothered about Ada, too. She looked pale and wilted, and had none of her usual sparkle. He ought to join her in the restaurant and try to reassure her, cheer her up. Only, he couldn't. He was too flat himself. That absurd wedding, and then the night he'd had. Best thing was to go back to the lounge and finish his drink.

Judge Meeklyn had been joined by Doc Paunders and Mr. Hernand, and Richard's drink stood on their table in front of an empty chair. He felt more like being alone, but supposed it would be rude, and dropped resignedly into the chair.

They were in the midst of a heated discussion, and ignored him. The judge contended that Miss Violet could have gone out of her mind, Doc Paunders said it was possible but not probable, and Mr. Hernand flatly declared that such a theory was not to be considered.

"She is one of the sanest women I have ever known."

"Which isn't saying much," Doc Paunders observed. "You've known so few women."

Mr. Hernand went pink with anger. "A bachelor gets to know far more women during the course of his life than you married men!"

"The average bachelor, yes," Judge Meeklyn nodded, "but not one like you." He laughed heartily, and Doc Paunders joined him.

Mr. Hernand drained his glass, stood up, and walked off after murmuring some sort of a chilly farewell.

"You hurt his feelings," Doc said. "Now he won't have lunch with us."

"I said nothing to hurt his feelings."

"Yes, you did. In fact, you're one of the most tactless old fools

I've ever known. Isn't he, Richard?"

Richard hadn't been listening, and he muttered automatically, "Yes."

The judge banged his glass wrathfully and stood up. "Very well, you two courteous people can have a polite lunch together. I'll take my crude tongue elsewhere."

"What are you getting excited about?" Doc demanded. "I didn't mean to make you sore."

"Oh no, you never mean these things. I can remember only a short while ago your telling Miss Dedingham that she was a copycat."

22

Richard looked up as judge Meeklyn marched off. He had heard his last remark, and he said a little vaguely, "What's the matter with him?"

Doc Paunders ordered another drink. "Touchy."

"Oh." Richard forgot about his lunch and stood up. "I'll be getting along."

He went out to his car and drove first to the funeral home for some necessary arrangements, and then out to the little house. Small groups of people were standing outside the fence, talking and staring, and a couple of the chief's men were on guard.

They refused to let him in. They explained that they had been stationed there to keep people from entering, and the chief had mentioned no exceptions. Richard tried to persuade one of them to go in and search for a photograph of Miss Ivy and was told that they, themselves, were not permitted inside.

He returned to his car and drove to the big house, where he went in at the back door. Annie was in the kitchen, and she greeted him with reserve, since she was afraid he might ask her to get him something to eat.

He did. The sight of the pantry reminded him that he had had no lunch, and Annie sighed and started to bang pots and the coffee percolator onto the stove. He left her and began to roam through the rooms of the ground floor, looking for a picture of Miss Ivy and keeping an eye out for the person of Miss Violet.

He found neither, and presently Annie called to him, and he returned to the kitchen. Pat was seated at the table, eating in silence, and his own place was laid opposite. He sat down and asked Annie if she could locate a picture of Miss Ivy.

"Sure, there's one in the liberry. Eat your lunch, and I'll go get it."

She returned with a small, framed photograph of a rather prim-looking young girl and put it down on the table. Richard had seen it in the library without remotely connecting it with Miss Ivy, but Annie vouched for the identity. He shook his head a little, but since he had nothing better he put it in his pocket.

After lunch he drove straight to the antique shop, and was given a chilly reception by the lady proprietor. She made it clear that she did not want him in her shop, and opened her thin lips long enough to tell him that she had given all that information to the police, who were the proper authorities.

Richard saw that his aunts' Royal tea set was still there, and on an inspiration he offered to buy it. The ice melted at once, and the woman studied the photograph of Miss Ivy with great care.

"Well, of course it's very difficult, isn't it? I mean, I really couldn't say whether this picture could be that woman in her youth. People change so over the years, don't they?"

Richard admitted it. "But at least you can tell me whether she was thin or stout."

"Oh, medium. I'm not really sure. She wore a heavy, black coat."

"Was it trimmed with fur?"

"I don't seem to remember, but if it was, the fur was black."

"Did she come in a car?"

The woman gave a refined little laugh. "I did notice that. It was such a *very* ancient electric."

Richard thanked her and started out of the shop, but at the door he stopped and turned. "I suppose she was driving it herself?"

"No. A man was driving. But the way the car was parked, out there, I saw only his legs, so there's no use asking me to describe *him*."

Richard gritted his teeth for a moment, and then asked, "What color were the trousers?"

"I don't know. Darkish."

Richard went off, carrying the tea set, which had been carefully wrapped and packed in a cardboard box. He placed it on the back seat of the car, and drove back to town at a furious pace.

Mrs. Evans was nearly hysterical and informed him that her heart simply would not stand the strain. Had he forgotten the afternoon session in court?

He had not, and contrary to his expectations, it went better than the morning session. Afterward, he returned to his office for a while, and it was after six when he finished at last and went to the street for his car.

So Miss Dedingham was a copycat? Maybe she tried to look like Miss Ivy.

Miss Ivy, he thought, would never have taken a man with her when she went to sell her china, but even supposing she had, most certainly she would not have allowed a man to drive her electric. Richard was the only man who had ever driven it, and that because she had intended leaving it to him in her will and thought he should learn to handle it. He considered Annie as the woman in the black coat, and shook his head. Pat couldn't drive any car, and most surely would never have put a foot in the electric. So what other man would drive Annie, even if she had any chance of borrowing the ancient vehicle? He frowned. Who else would have a chance of borrowing the thing, anyhow? Well, Miss Violet, of course, and she'd probably be able to get a man to drive it for her. But Miss Violet never wore a cameo pin. He'd often heard her say that she disliked cameos. More important than that, she did not need money, and she, in common with Miss Ivy, considered their possessions to be sacred.

So it had to be Miss Dedingham. She needed money badly, and she had access to both the aunts' houses. On such a mission she would almost certainly wear a forbidding expression, she had graying hair, and it was probable that she possessed a cameo pin and a nondescript black coat. She was heavier than Miss Ivy, but the description of medium weight under a coat gave a lot of ground either way.

He drove to Judge Meeklyn's home, and went in to find the judge absorbed with the evening newspaper. He raised his head with an inquiring look, and Richard said directly, "I believe I've found out who sold that tea set belonging to my aunts. It was Miss Deding-ham."

He was quite unprepared for the outburst of fury that greeted this statement, and for a while he was unable to make himself heard at all, even though he was attempting to soothe. Coherent speech even-tually returned. "To whom have you dared mention this base suspi-cion?"

"Nobody," Richard said hastily. "Not a soul but yourself, and I don't think it's a base suspicion. I regard it as a fact. She's more like a sister to my aunts than a friend, and since she needs money so badly they might have given, or perhaps she thought they intended to give, er—"

"Good God, man, what are you talking about?" the judge thun-dered. "Miss Dedingham is financially sound. She doesn't need money from anyone."

"Oh, come off it," Richard said impatiently. "Everyone in town knows she's broke."

"No, no." Judge Meeklyn thumped the arm of his chair. "She likes to give that impression, that's all. Actually, she has enough."

Richard decided to let it go. He said pacifically, "I see, yes. I didn't mean to accuse her. As I say, I more or less regard her as one of my aunts. Have you seen her today? I think I'll go over there now. I hope she's better."

"Better? What do you mean?"

He didn't know. There'd been so many other things that Miss Dedingham's illness was almost forgotten.

Judge Meeklyn pulled on his topcoat and buttoned it up so that there was an odd buttonhole at the bottom and an odd button at the top.

"You won't need your coat," Richard said. "It's much warmer. After all, it's almost May."

The judge stamped out without bothering to reply, and they went to Miss Dedingham's house in a heavy silence.

They were met in the front hall by a nurse who said that Miss Dedingham was much better. "But she seems very disturbed about my being here. She wants me to go."

The judge brushed by and headed straight for Miss Dedingham's bedroom, and the nurse followed, protesting. Richard crept after both of them on the tips of his toes.

Miss Dedingham's eyes were open, and they followed the judge as he sat down in a chair by her bed. Her mouth worked a little, and she said, "It was awful. She looked at her dead sister and moved those chairs the way she wanted them."

23

Judge Meeklyn held Miss Dedingham's hand and said gently, "It's all right, you must not worry about anything. I'm right here beside you and you can leave everything to me."

Miss Dedingham closed her eyes and seemed to go to sleep. Richard lingered, but she said nothing more, and he knew she must have seen the chairs being moved. He glanced at the faces of the judge and the nurse, and they did not appear to be startled or surprised, and the nurse presently slipped quietly out of the room with a murmur about some errand.

Richard moved over to the dresser. He eyed the top drawer, and then gave a quick look over his shoulder and pulled it open. To his horror, it gave a protesting squeak, and Judge Meeklyn turned his head. Richard took a backward step and stared steadily at Miss Dedingham.

Judge Meeklyn said, "Shh!" and picked up Miss Dedingham's limp hand again, and after a suitable interval Richard returned to the dresser. The drawer contained a tumbled mess of things, and he burrowed cautiously. It took a little time, but he found the cameo at last, in a small box. It was exactly like the one Miss Ivy wore, so much so, in fact, that he wondered if it were the same brooch. Had Miss Ivy worn it lately? He tried to remember, but it had always been so much a part of her that he had long since ceased to notice it. He replaced it in the box and closed the drawer. The judge turned again, sharply, and Richard muttered, "Sorry."

The judge sternly motioned him from the room, and he went out, feeling like a bad little boy. He had looked around for a closet in there, and had not found one. It was the old library, of course, which

Miss Dedingham had used for a bedroom when she moved down-stairs, but he had thought she might have furnished it with an old-fashioned wardrobe, or something of that sort. But there was noth-ing, and he had to assume that she kept her clothes somewhere out-side.

He did not have far to look. There was a closet in the hall, directly outside, and he found Miss Dedingham's few, shabby garments hang-ing there. One of them was a black coat trimmed with short, black fur, and after looking at it for a moment he backed out and shut the door. Pathetic, somehow, but he had to go on and find the man who'd been with her. One thing was certain, though. He wouldn't tell the chief. Let him go on thinking that Miss Ivy had been selling her own stuff.

An encouraging smell of coffee took him to the kitchen, where he found the nurse sitting at a table over her dinner. She stopped chew-ing long enough to say, "I'm glad that you gentlemen arrived. She's coming around slowly now, and I haven't been able to leave."

"How bad is she?" Richard asked.

"Not bad at all. She seems pretty good to me."

"Do you think she'll make a complete recovery?"

She retreated into professionalism and said, "You'll have to ask the doctor."

"Has she been talking much?"

"No."

"What else has she said, besides what I heard just now?"

"Nothing much, but you don't have to worry, because I have to tell everything she says to Chief O'Brien. He thinks maybe she knows something about that murder, and *wasn't* that awful? I'm telling you, I was glad to see you gentlemen, and I can't stay here alone tonight. I've been waiting for Dr. Paunders to tell him so."

"When is he coming?"

She shrugged in the manner of a nurse who was well accustomed to the vagaries of doctors' comings and goings. "He said he'd be early."

There was a sound from the front hall, and they both went out to find Mr. Hernand removing his hat. "I knocked," he stated primly, "before I came in."

"That's all right, Mr. Hernand," the nurse said. "But I guess Miss

Dedingham never locked that door. I tried, and found that it just won't catch."

"I've always walked straight in," Richard said thoughtfully. "I never remember it being locked."

Mr. Hernand nodded. "She never heard if you knocked. We always walked in. How is she?"

"Pretty good," the nurse told him cheerfully. "Judge Meeklyn is with her."

"Ah, yes. I was taking my evening walk, and decided to look in and see whether I could be of any help."

"There is a problem," Richard said. "Nurse doesn't want to stay here alone tonight. I don't know whether the judge would be willing to stay, or whether you could. Doc Paunders is expected soon, so perhaps the three of you could come to some arrangement. I have to get on home, now, but if you need any help, let me know."

"No need of that, I'm sure." Mr. Hernand was moving toward the bedroom. "We, her friends, will see to her welfare."

Richard returned to his car and made off for the big house as quickly as possible. It was after eight, and he'd had no dinner, and it occurred to him that either Ada or Annie might have prepared a meal for him. In fact, Ada might be annoyed, since he hadn't even phoned.

He put the car away in the garage and walked to the back door. In the kitchen he found Annie seated at the table drumming her fingers and looking distinctly put out.

"I hope you weren't waiting dinner for me. I had things to do."

"It ain't you," Annie told him austerely. "I ain't onea them strait-laced old sourpusses, but there's a limit. As for the dinner, that was ruined hours ago, and as for me, I'm only the help. It don't matter what time *I* get to bed, I'm sure."

"I'm sorry. I suppose she's waiting for me?"

"Sure," Annie said sulkily. "Not she. They."

Richard raised his eyebrows and went on to the library to see who "they" were.

He found Madge and Ada sitting in an atmosphere that had frost around the edges, and he was conscious of a peculiar sense of embarrassment which became acute when Madge raised her head and looked at him. He reminded himself that he had never gone beyond taking her out occasionally through the years, and most certainly he had never led her to believe that he meant anything serious, and yet her eyes silently accused him of having thrown her out into the snow.

Ada was carefully polite. "We thought you were never coming, Richard. Madge is staying for dinner. You can drive her home later. I'll tell Annie we're ready."

She left, walking gracefully, and Richard tried to move his tongue and found that it was stuck.

"Richard." Madge's voice was low and intimate. "I know you did a very gallant thing when you married Ada, under the circumstances, but you didn't consider me very much, did you?"

Richard said, "But—" and Ada appeared at the door and coldly announced that dinner was ready.

They went to the dining room and sat down in silence, and Annie came in and slapped a few things onto the table.

"You can't keep food fit to eat by leaving it in the oven after it's cooked. I got a reputation with my cookin' and it makes me sore to hand out swill like this. When I'm told to get dinner ready that's the time it's ready, right then, and no later."

She left the room, and Richard said, "It's getting warmer, I believe."

Ada said, "*Really?*"

Madge coughed. "I'm so glad. I do like a nice spring."

"How's your mother, Madge?" Richard asked.

"Very well, thank you," Ada said courteously.

Madge gave her a look. "I believe it was *my* mother he inquired for."

"It was, but since you've already told me how she is, I thought I'd save you the trouble."

Madge compressed her lips, and Richard essayed a laugh which he regretted at once.

There were noises of arrival from the direction of the kitchen, and Mrs. Balron presently walked in. She looked at the three of them and stopped short.

"What's this? I suppose I'm old-fashioned, but it seems odd for a man to take his ex-girlfriend along on his honeymoon."

Richard blushed, and Ada said, "What makes you think she's ex?"

Madge gave Richard a look of wistful appeal, and he said, "It's even odder for a man to take his mother along on his honeymoon, isn't it?"

"No, it's more dull, that's all. What's the matter with you, anyway, crowding all these people into a honeymoon? You're a rotten bridegroom, and if it were me, I wouldn't put up with it."

"Please, Mrs. Balron!" Madge whispered. "All this joking! It— it's not in the best taste."

"Who's joking?" Mrs. Balron demanded. "My son should take his bride away where they can be alone, instead of being bothered by people like you and me."

Madge flushed and stiffened her spine. "I did not come here to *bother* them. I had something very important to say to Ada."

"Very important indeed," Ada murmured.

Madge gave her a suspicious glance, and Richard asked, "Have you had dinner, Mother? Would you like to sit down and—"

"Of course I've had dinner. It's late."

"You must have an errand, Mrs. Balron," Madge said gently. "I know you wouldn't, er, bother these two, otherwise."

"Don't ever mix sarcasm and syrup, Madge," Mrs. Balron said abstractedly, "it leaves such a bad smell around you. Richard, the chief wants to see you. He's convinced that one of those old men is hiding Miss Violet in his house."

24

Richard sipped coffee and squinted at his mother. "Maybe he's right, at that, but I don't know why he wants to see me."

"They're all over at Miss Dedingham's," Mrs. Balron said. "I dropped in to see how she was, and the chief took me to one side and asked me to go for you. He's trying to get them to let him search their houses, and they won't have it."

"What makes him think I'd try to persuade them? He accused me of attempting to hide her, too."

"Maybe he's being smarter than you think," Mrs. Balron suggested. "He might figure that you'll go right over, now, and look through their houses by yourself, to get her before he does. It would never surprise me to find that he has someone tailing you. He's police, so he can't look through their musty old houses without their consent, but he'd love to have you sneak around and do the job for him."

Richard nodded thoughtfully. "Only I'll fool him. I'll go straight to Miss Dedingham's and help with the persuading. I want her found, and I think I can put enough pressure on the chief so that he won't arrest her. I'll bring her back here."

"Fine. Maybe Madge and I could stay here too, and perhaps the chief would like a room so that he can keep an eye on Miss Violet."

Madge stood up and said thinly, "I must be going."

"Richard." Ada glanced at him. "Suppose you drive Madge home before you go to Miss Dedingham's."

"I'll be glad to drive her home," Mrs. Balron said.

Madge gave a little gasp. "Oh *no!*"

Richard grinned. "She's scared to drive with you, and I don't blame her. Come on, Madge, I'll take you over now."

They all went out together. Ada's face was forbidding. Richard felt uncomfortable. Madge was smiling. Mrs. Balron waved the car away cheerfully, and then returned to the kitchen door, where Ada was standing.

"May I have a chat with you, my dear?"

Ada nodded briefly and turned to lead the way through the kitchen. They went on to the library, where Ada sprawled in a chair and stared at nothing. Mrs. Balron settled herself comfortably and said, "Now! I must know what Madge wanted, coming here like that."

"Why must you know?"

"Out of curiosity," Mrs. Balron said simply.

"Oh, well, then I suppose I'd better tell you. She came to be completely frank and help in what she called 'the mess.' "

"She did?"

"Yes. She said she knew Richard had married me to help me out of some trouble, since she and Richard had had an understanding that they were to be married sometime."

Mrs. Balron nodded. "No hurry, just sometime. She hoped. He might have, too, out of desperation."

"How do you know it would have been desperation?"

"She's been available for quite some time," Mrs. Balron said mildly.

"I see."

"So, what *did* you marry him for?"

Ada stood up and said, "I'm a fool!"

"I think that offends me, somewhat. My son is a catch."

Ada turned around on her. "He had no right to drive her home when you were there to do it."

"Rubbish! He merely wants to flirt with her a little. She keeps asking for it, and he's human. Listen, how did she intend to help?"

"She said if we intended to get a divorce as soon as possible, she'd wait for Richard, but if not, she would arrange her life differently."

"What did you say?"

"I said I really didn't know, and that she'd better wait a few weeks and then come and visit me again."

"That's reasonable," Mrs. Balron agreed. "What did she say to that?"

"She turned nasty. She nodded her rabbity little nose up and down and said that she could understand I'd need a little time to try and make him."

Mrs. Balron laughed heartily, and Ada began to pace the room with short, nervous steps.

Mrs. Balron left shortly afterwards, and on her way home passed Richard, who was heading for Miss Dedingham's. He was wondering if the chief would still be there, and was relieved to find him when he arrived. The nurse was moving about quietly, but there was no sign of Miss Violet's three beaux.

"You wanted to see me?" Richard asked abruptly.

The chief nodded. "What took you so long?"

Richard explained about Madge, and the chief fiddled with his lower lip. "You sure that's what you been doing?"

"I'm sure that's what I been doing. Where are the three gents?" Richard asked.

"In with Miss Dedingham. She's better."

"Are they all talking to her?"

The nurse, who had appeared from the direction of the kitchen, assumed a nurse's look of disapproval and spoke primly. "I cannot understand why Dr. Paunders permits it, those two talking with her, there, when she should have absolute quiet."

The chief flung her a glance. "Ahh, you nurses fuss too much. What's wrong with them sitting with her, when they're the closest things she's got to relatives?"

"Have they agreed to let you search their houses?" Richard asked.

"They have not and they never will and they'll sue me if I put a foot on any of their porches."

The nurse said, "I don't blame them."

The chief turned on her. "Haven't you got duties? Somewhere else? Like taking care of your patient?"

She had seated herself with a lapful of yellow knitting, but she gathered it up again and walked off with her head in the air.

The chief sighed deeply and muttered, "I been trying to get rid of her for some time." He went quietly to Miss Dedingham's door and laid his ear against it.

Richard followed and stood close beside him.

Mr. Hernand was speaking. "—as I said before, if he forces the issue, we can bolt our doors and stay inside."

"It's not a matter of bolting our doors," Judge Meeklyn said impatiently. "It's merely a matter of upholding our *rights*."

Doc Paunders snorted. "He won't bother us any more. He knows he's out of line, so what are we worrying about? Be something, wouldn't it, we three having our houses searched? The whole town would know about it, and we'd be suspected of all the crimes in the book."

Miss Dedingham said, "I'll get up tomorrow."

Judge Meeklyn sighed. "She should have come to one of us instead of wandering off somewhere."

"Do you think she wandered off into the woods?" Doc asked.

"No." Mr. Hernand sounded tired. "What little woods we have have been searched thoroughly by the police."

"Ahh, the police!" Doc sneered.

"The police are doing a fine job," Judge Meeklyn declared. "But of course they have no right to want to search our homes."

Miss Dedingham spoke again. "Ivy was a bit nasty, at times, but you should not have hit her like that."

25

The chief put the flat of his hand on the door, swung it open, and stalked in. He glared briefly at the three men, and then went over to the bed.

"Miss Dedingham, which one of these men hit Miss Ivy?"

Miss Dedingham's eyes had been hazy, but they narrowed and focused on the face above her. "My good man," she said clearly, "be kind enough to remove yourself from my house."

The chief opened his mouth to try again, but Doc Paunders spoke up with authority. "You must leave immediately, Chief. My patient is in no condition for questioning."

He urged him to the door, where the chief made a last stand. "She saw the murder of Miss Ivy. I want to know—this is a murder investigation—"

"My dear fellow," said Doc Paunders, "she is not rational. She may have seen something, or heard someone talking, around here, but whatever it is, you'll have to wait until she's well enough for your questions."

Richard stepped away from the door as the chief came out and watched him in silence as he fumed up and down the room. When he had blown off some of the steam he turned to Richard and said, "I can't stay here all night. I got things to do. You see what you can do to get those three stubborn mules to let me search their houses, and if two say yes, and one no, tell me right away, and I'll act."

He stamped off, and Richard turned back to Miss Dedingham's room. The bedroom door was ajar, and he moved forward and peered in. Mr. Hernand and Judge Meeklyn were standing at one side of the bed, and Doc Paunders and the nurse stood at the other. Miss Dedingham's eyes were open, and Doc Paunders was speaking to her in a low voice.

"—and she changed those chairs?"

Miss Dedingham moved her head on the pillow, and her words

came out in an odd slur. "Yes, she changed them. It was awful, awful. Violet always—"

Doc Paunders shifted his weight. "It wasn't so bad *then*. I know Violet *never* would change those chairs."

"No, never, never, never—"

"But you saw it. It must have been remorse. When it was too late she put the chair where her sister had always wanted it."

Judge Meeklyn nodded solemnly, and the nurse and Mr. Hernand followed suit. Richard looked at their faces and thought that they were quite ready to believe that Miss Violet had killed her sister, but he still could not accept it himself.

Doc Paunders patted Miss Dedingham's hand, said something in an undertone to the nurse, and then motioned Mr. Hernand and Judge Meeklyn out of the room. Richard went with them, and they seemed unaware that there were more of them going out than had come in.

Judge Meeklyn ran a worried hand through his hair and muttered, "She must have seen what happened."

Mr. Hernand shook his head sadly, and the judge added, "She must have had a terrible experience."

"Did she say anything about Aunt Violet's whereabouts?" Richard asked.

They looked at him vaguely and shook their heads, and then turned as Doc Paunders came out of the bedroom.

"I've given her something to make her sleep. I'd been hoping she could tell us about last night, but she's just repeating the same thing over and over again. Often happens in these cases. We'll simply have to wait."

"Will she be all right?" Judge Meeklyn asked anxiously. "Is she better?"

Doc Paunders nodded. "She's better. But you can't tell with these strokes. She might have another—no certainty about her recovery— her heart. Anyway, we can only hope for the best."

Mr. Hernand sighed and stirred. "Nurse won't stay here alone tonight, Doc. One of us will have to stay with her."

"Er, yes. Well, I'm afraid I can't—another patient. I, er—"

"I'll stay," Richard said. "I'm dead tired now. I'll sleep on the couch in the hall, here."

Mr. Hernand made a vexed sound with his tongue. "Certainly not.

You are newly married and your place is with your bride. You can't leave her in that great empty house by herself. I shall stay."

"No, no," Judge Meeklyn protested. "You go now, Hernand. You know I couldn't leave. I'm staying in any case, so the rest of you might as well get some repose."

Doc Paunders had his own car, but Richard drove Mr. Hernand home and then went on to the big house. He parked his car close to the back door, where light was streaming out.

Ada was sitting at the kitchen table, drinking coffee. She glanced up at him and said, "There's coffee in the pot if you want some, but I should think you'd prefer to sleep."

Richard much preferred to sleep, but simple perversity sent him to the stove to pour coffee.

"I'll be leaving in the morning," Ada told him. "I had no idea you were already engaged when you married me."

He drank too-hot coffee in dignified silence, and had to recover himself before he asked distantly, "Have you seen Aunt Violet?"

"No, but I might have heard her. I heard somebody or something down here. I was scared, but I came down and looked around, and even called into the cellar."

"You didn't go down into the cellar?"

"No, I'm afraid to go there, especially at night. I've been waiting for you to come back to tell you to go and investigate. If you're afraid too, I'll go down with you."

"Thank you," said Richard, "but I am not afraid."

"Good." She stood up. "Good night, and good-by. I won't be seeing you in the morning."

She left the room, and he took another, and more careful, sip of coffee. He really had no idea that he was engaged to Madge until she told him so on the way to her home tonight. Whatever had become of the old formal proposals, anyway?

The coffee had revived him a little, and he went to the back hall and down to the cellar. The lighting was poor, but he went into every dim corner, and found exactly nothing. It seemed incredible that Miss Violet could elude them like this, but he'd done everything, looked everywhere. What more could he do? He was desperately tired, and Ada's annoyance bothered him. He'd have to get some sleep before he could think clearly or do anything more.

He climbed slowly to the second floor and had just reached the top when Ada burst out of her room. She stopped when she saw him, and then circled around and started down the stairs. "I've just thought of something. Maybe I'm wrong, but I want to see."

He followed her, walking like a somnambulist, and she went to the library and over to one of the windows.

"I thought so. See?"

Richard looked down at a small table. A vase stood on top, and it held four artificial black iris.

26

Richard looked at the vase with eyes that seemed to be filled with sand, and muttered, "So what about it?"

"So nothing." Ada turned her back on him and left the room.

Richard went to bed. As he dragged his clothes off he thought vaguely that something should be done about the vase of flowers, only he didn't quite know what. He was asleep the instant he stretched out, despite the two cups of coffee.

Ada waited at her door until sounds from his room had ceased, and then she slipped out. She went down the hall to the stairs that led to the attic, and stood there for a moment, hesitating. She wanted to have a look at the blue and red leather books in the secret room. She hadn't told Richard about them, but she half wished, now, that she'd asked him to come with her. No use dithering, anyway. Might as well get it over with.

She switched on the light, and went up the stairs. It had occurred to her that the books might be diaries, which would explain how the aunts spent their time in that room and why they always kept it locked. She thought it possible, too, that Miss Violet was hiding there. She had surely been in the house a little while ago, since the paper flowers had not been in the library earlier.

The hall was dim and empty, and she glanced back at the stairs and shivered. She wanted to go down and get back to the safety of her room, but she must look, now that she was up here—and Richard sleeping like a pig, as though nothing were wrong! Well, no, that wasn't fair. He'd had no sleep, and had been in court all day.

Aunt Violet must be up in the attic now, frightened or ill. She'd look through all the rooms, even though she was scared.

The light switches were on the walls at the doors, and she had no trouble in her swift search of the rooms. She came at last to the one that had the closet with the door at the back, and she was conscious of her heart thudding uncomfortably. She was afraid of that little, secret apartment, so empty and quiet, and so typical of the two sisters.

She pushed through the closet and pressed the panels of the farther door with sweating palms. It swung away from her, and she looked into darkness that was filtered with moonlight from the window, but the two chairs were in shadow. She groped frantically for a switch and could not find one, and she began to have a chilling feeling that the chairs were occupied. Miss Ivy, dreadfully hacked and dead in the red chair—Miss Violet, with mad laughter bubbling on her lips in the blue.

Ada gave a little gasp, and her searching hand dropped away from the wall. She stumbled forward, groped for the books, and snatched them from their tables without looking at the chairs. She was breathing hard as she fled back through the closet, and she hurried down the stairs, clutching the two books tightly against her chest. She made a hasty search of her room before locking all the doors, and then got into bed with the pillows propped behind her and lighted a cigarette with shaking fingers. Surely no one had been sitting in the chairs? Of course not. She'd gone into a silly panic, that was all—too much imagination.

The books were diaries, all right, but they were locked, and there were no keys. She wouldn't believe it, at first, as she twitched and pulled impatiently, but the books were expensive and well made, and the locks held fast.

She closed her eyes for a moment and swore softly, and then her head jerked up from the pillow as she thought she heard someone coming up the stairs. Was it a sound of footsteps? But there were so many noises in this old place, and she was nervous enough to imagine anything. She listened with straining ears to silence, and frowned impatiently at herself. It was absurd to be so jumpy.

She got out of bed and rummaged among her things in search of a small key, and presently found two. One belonged to her jewel case and the other to a small suitcase, but neither would fit the diaries, although she turned and twisted frantically.

She thought, now, that she heard someone mounting the attic stairs, but she was cross and exasperated with the locks and with herself, and she determinedly closed her ears. It was weak and silly to keep on imagining things just because the house was old and full of odd noises.

The locks of the diaries were fastened to broad, leather straps that were attached to the backs of the books. She had no scissors, but she tried for a while to cut a strap with her toenail clippers. The short blades scratched and chewed at the leather, but they would not cut it, and she presently threw the clippers aside in a temper.

She *must* read these books. The contents might be terribly important. She'd have to go down to the kitchen. There'd be knives there, and perhaps scissors as well. She gathered the books under her arm and slowly approached the door. She knew that she was frightened, but her interest in the diaries urged her on, and after she had unlocked the door she flew downstairs and along to the kitchen. It was better there than in the shadowy halls, and she found a pair of scissors almost at once. They were very large, and the blade would not fit under the strap, so she presently flung them down and went to get a knife. She hacked for a while at the blue book, which she knew belonged to Miss Violet, but the knife proved to be little better than the scissors.

She needed a smaller pair of scissors, and the place to look was the desk in the library. She hated to leave the cheerful kitchen, but she was obsessed, by now, with a determination to read the diaries, and she crept through the butler's pantry and the dining room and into the library. The arch that led to the hall was hung with heavy drapes, and she looked at them fearfully and wished that she had the courage to fling them aside and assure herself that there was no one in the hall. She turned her back on the arch and moved over to the desk.

There was someone coming down the stairs. She was not mistaken this time. She couldn't be. She tried to listen and seemed to hear only the muffled pounding of her heart, and then she heard the click of the front door closing.

She could not move. Someone had gone out, or come in. A dim figure in that vast hall, approaching the drapes. Aunt Violet, with her mind wandering and her eyes mad and empty. Aunt Ivy, thudding on dead legs with her face hacked to pieces …

The drapes parted, and Ada screamed shrilly. Richard came in, knotting the belt of his robe, and she stared at him wildly with her hand crushed against her mouth.

"What is it? What's the matter?"

"Oh." Ada dropped her hand and felt a sagging of her whole body. "I— Did you just come in the front door?"

"No. I heard a noise of some sort. It woke me up, so I got out of bed, and when I saw your door open I came down."

"Then someone just went out."

Richard went to the front door, opened it, and looked out. He could see nothing, and he presently returned to the library and said a little impatiently, "I can't see anything. What are you doing here, anyway?"

Ada told him and added, "I can't sleep while Aunt Violet is still missing."

"So you want to snoop in her diary?"

Ada stiffened her spine and said, "Why don't you go back to bed?"

"I suppose you think you'll find something in the diary that will lead you to where she is now."

"I might, so let's leave it at that."

She turned back to the desk and began to rummage furiously, and after a moment he asked, "What are you looking for?"

"A pair of scissors."

"May I ask why?"

Ada found the scissors at that point, and she marched back to the kitchen without bothering to reply.

Richard followed in silence, but when he saw her attempt to cut the leather strap on the blue diary he let out a yell.

Ada dropped the scissors and then cried peevishly, "What *is* the matter with you?"

"You're ruining the book! Here, give it to me. I'll take the lock off, and then it can be put on again without any damage."

Ada handed the diary to him sulkily and asked, "Why don't you find out who just left by way of the front door?"

"Nobody just left by way of the front door. You're nervous and hysterical, and you're hearing things." He had a tool of some sort and was prying up the small, gilt plate that surrounded the lock.

"Do you think it was my hysterical imagination that woke you up?" Ada demanded.

"It was your running around the house that woke me up."

"Oh no." She shook her head. "I made no sound at all, but when the front door was opened and closed it *did* make a sound."

Richard eased the metal plate from the diary and, after carelessly riffling through the pages, handed it over to her. "There you are. I suppose you want to find out about their boyfriends."

It was exactly what she'd had in mind, and she received the book in silence.

"At that, I suppose we might turn up a clue, that way."

Ada was turning the pages eagerly. It was Miss Violet's, all right, written in a small, neat hand, and she turned to the last entry and looked at the date.

She stared at it and said in a dazed voice, "But that's the date of today."

27

Richard said, "Yesterday, actually. It's after twelve." He tried to draw the book toward him, but Ada clutched it firmly, and he was obliged to look at it over her shoulder.

"I cannot live, now that my world has fallen apart, but I must finish my diary before I die. I have swallowed a quantity of pills all together, and I am waiting for them to put an end to me.

"Today I saw my darling Ada married. It should have been a happy time, but after the guests had left, we had a bitter quarrel. In the end, we arranged to play our game six times, and if one of us were killed, the other might have her way. If both survived, we would take our dispute to Richard, and each would have a chance to talk.

"We prepared for the game, and Ivy said that since we had no luck so far, we should switch guns—I to take hers, and she to take mine. The third time we tried, hers went off, and a bullet seemed to go right through my head. I believe it just brushed my hair, but I thought I had been mortally wounded, and I sank to the ground. I was lying there, dazed and helpless, she looked down at me, and *moved those chairs* to where she had always wanted them. She thought I was dead, and she couldn't wait. Horrible!

"I heard someone rush into the room, and Ivy screamed, and it brought me to my senses a little. I opened my eyes wider and saw my dear friend holding the little hatchet, the one we keep at the fireplace to chop twigs. He raised it, and Ivy ran from him. She went down to the cellar, and he was after her, screaming at her. She screamed only once, poor Ivy, and I heard him tell her, over and over again, how she had ruined the chance of a marriage between him and myself. I am sure, though, and it comforts me, that she died very quickly and did not hear all the dreadful things he said to her.

"I was terrified. I managed to crawl out through the door, and on the porch I staggered to my feet, and ran over here to the big house. I was not quite in my right senses, I think. I seemed to hear him coming after me with that hideous hatchet, and I screamed with what little breath I had. I could not get in to the big house, and it was raining and blowing. I cried and moaned, trying to get them to hear me, and I ran around and around the house, and then at last there was a light at the back door, and I went in. I was afraid he would come after me, so I ran straight up here to the attic, and it was in the bathroom, here, that I found the pills.

"I didn't want him to find me and lead me away. I couldn't go with him, no. He is a murderer, and I cannot see him again. I shall sit here quietly until the pills put me to sleep forever."

Ada drew a shuddering breath, and Richard said abruptly, "I'll phone the chief right away. This should clear Aunt Violet for him."

He went to the library, and Ada got up and tried the back door. It was unlocked, and she turned the key with a quick, nervous movement. Perhaps the front door was unlocked too. She'd heard someone go out. She went through to the front hall, but the door was locked there. She could find no bolt, but the lock fastened automatically for the outside.

Richard came out of the library. "I'm going up to see what sort of pills she took. I suppose she left the bottle there."

Ada nodded. "Is the chief coming?"

"No. Said he'd be around the first thing in the morning. What did you do with the diary?"

"It's in the kitchen. I'll get it. If you'll open Aunt Ivy's book for me, I'll read them both, and perhaps I can find out who Aunt Violet's 'dear friend' is."

"I wish you would," Richard said. "I know you haven't had much sleep, but I don't believe I could keep my eyes open even for that."

He removed the lock from Miss Ivy's diary, and then went off to the attic.

Richard found that the medicine chest in the attic bathroom contained only a box of bandages and an empty bottle. The bottle had held aspirin, but he had no way of knowing how many she had taken nor any idea on fatal doses of aspirin. He shrugged and returned to the second floor. Her mind had been clear when she wrote in the diary, and it seemed probable that a few aspirin tablets wouldn't do her any harm. She'd intended to stay in this house, and yet she had left, and had picked Pat's fake iris, brought them in, and put them in a vase. Should he start searching the whole house again? He shook his head. She wasn't here now. She was with one of her friends, and the chances were that she was all right.

Ada opened her door and looked out at him. "Did you find out what sort of pills she took?"

"All I found was an empty aspirin bottle. Have you dug up anything in the diaries yet?"

"Not yet. I'm going to read more now."

She retired into her room and locked the door, and Richard headed for his bed.

Ada was soon deep in Miss Violet's diary. It was interesting in a way, but there was a lot of repetition. She would write faithfully every day for a while, and then would drop it for months at a time. She'd had three beaux, Judge Meeklyn, Doc Paunders and Mr. Hernand, and all of them apparently anxious to marry her. But Miss Violet seemed evasive about marriage. Her earlier excuse was that her father did not wish it, and after his death she stated, several times, that she could not leave her sister. Poor Ivy would be all alone.

When Ada finished at last she was as much in the dark as ever as to which of the three men was the "dear friend." She put the book aside, and then discovered that she did not have Miss Ivy's diary. Richard had said he'd take the books up for her on his way to the attic, but apparently he'd left the red one in the kitchen. Nothing for it but to go on down again and get it. She looked at her watch and saw that it was six o'clock and decided that she might as well have some breakfast before she started on Miss Ivy's book. It hadn't taken too long to finish Aunt Violet's. She should get through the second one by about nine o'clock.

She went down to the kitchen and was exasperated to find that the book was not there. What *had* Richard done with it? Perhaps he'd taken it with him when he went to the attic with some idea of looking it over while she was busy with the other one. But he hadn't had it when he came down, so it seemed probable that he had left it up there.

Ada sighed and pulled her gown tightly around her. She hated that dim, silent, frightening place, but she *must* get Miss Ivy's diary. Anyway, it was light now, and even the attic would be more cheerful in the daytime.

She mounted slowly and went first to the bathroom, but Richard had not left the book there. She hesitated and knew that she would have to go to the secret room and reassure herself that no one was sitting in either of those chairs. She had really come up for that, and she knew it.

She moved forward on stiff legs, calling herself a fool, and yet unable to stop. She pushed nervously at the old coats in the closet, so that the hangers rattled, and opened the farther door just enough so that she might peer in.

Miss Violet sat in the blue chair, her dead eyes staring from under half-closed lids.

28

With no very clear idea of how she had got there Ada found herself in Richard's room, shaking his shoulder and whimpering entreaties at him to wake up. He did rouse at last, and blinked at her stupidly.

"Richard, it's Aunt Violet. She's *dead*."

He was out of bed in a single movement, and struggling into his robe. "Where is she? How do you know—"

"In the attic, in that room. Oh, please come!"

They went upstairs, and Ada urged him along the hall, but she would not go into the room again. She stood just outside, crying, with her arm across her eyes.

Miss Violet was dressed in the gown that she had worn to the wedding. Her head was thrown back a little, and she was already stiff and cold.

Richard said slowly, "I should have listened to you when you said you heard noises. She was dead when she was brought in here."

He came out into the hall and put an arm across Ada's shoulders. "Come on, we'll go down. We can't do anything here. I'll phone the chief again. He'll have to come now."

They went down, and Ada made her way to the kitchen while Richard telephoned. When he joined her he found her staring out of the window while something burned in a frying pan and the coffee bubbled over. He moved the pan and poured a cup of coffee and took it to her. "You'd better drink this."

She looked up at him.

Richard said, "I'll get Mother."

Mrs. Balron appeared in a remarkably short space of time, and she had Annie in tow. Annie's eyes were snapping with excitement as she tied an apron around her waist. "So them two finally battled it out to a finish! I knew something hadda happen sooner or later."

"You get us all some breakfast," Mrs. Balron said austerely. "Ada, my poor child, I know you were fond of her. With your parents both dead she was all you had. Unless you have some other relatives? Do you want me to send for anyone?" She put a competent arm around Ada and seemed cheerfully ready to attend to everything.

Ada shook her head. "Father never kept up with the relatives. I have some friends, but I don't want them now, if you'll stay with me for a while."

"Of course, as long as you need me. Richard! What are you standing around like a hooked fish for? Why don't you call the chief?"

"I did, but you couldn't expect him to get here before you."

"Oh. Well, no. His system is to linger just long enough for the criminal to escape."

The chief banged into the kitchen as she finished speaking, and several men crowded in behind him. Richard moved to lead them upstairs, and Mrs. Balron said to him from the corner of her mouth, "Come right down again and let him make his mistakes by himself. Annie'll have breakfast for you. The old fool will have to kill time by asking us questions while he thinks up what to do, so we might as well be fortified."

She told Annie to have breakfast on the table in five minutes, and led Ada to a seat at the dining-room table. Annie called after her that there wasn't nobody could get breakfast for three people in five minutes, and Mrs. Balron told her to do it anyway.

"I can't eat," Ada said despairingly.

"Yes, you can, and the sooner the better. This whole thing is bad, but it will pass, and it could be worse."

Richard did not return at once from the attic. He had a lot to tell the chief, and, in fact, when he did get back to the dining room the chief was with him. They both sat down at the table where Mrs. Balron and Ada were already eating.

The chief turned to Ada and asked furiously, "Why didn't you tell me about that secret room up there?"

She gave him a cold stare. "It's not a secret room, really. I found it, and I naturally assumed that you had, too. That's your business."

The chief colored darkly and went on to hint that Miss Violet had been up there all the time, and that Ada had tried to keep it from him.

Eventually he asked what had taken her to the attic so early in the morning, and she explained, "I couldn't find Aunt Ivy's diary, and I thought Richard might have taken it up there."

"I put them both in your room," Richard said.

Mrs. Balron suspended a fork and stared at him. "*Her* room? Aren't you occupying the same room, son?"

Richard looked at his mother and knew that he couldn't shut her up. He said stiffly, "No. Something came up which decided us to use separate rooms."

Mrs. Balron narrowed her eyes, and the chief grumbled, "You're lucky you got two rooms. Now my wife, when we got married she was in a great way to have separate rooms, but I guess we did better sticking it out. We didn't have two bedrooms, anyways."

Mrs. Balron murmured, "The poor woman."

Ada got up, murmured an excuse, and left the room. Mrs. Balron hastily finished her own breakfast and what was left of Ada's, which was most of it, and followed her.

She found her upstairs in her bedroom, sitting on the side of the bed, with Miss Ivy's diary on her lap.

"It was here all the time. It had fallen down behind the night table."

Mrs. Balron seated herself in an armchair and gazed about her. "Some fancy bedroom, huh? Only I think it would give me the creeps. I'd feel downright vulgar, cutting my toenails in a place like this."

Ada fingered the red diary and said, "I'd like to read this before the chief takes it. If I only had a little time, I'm sure I'd get more out of it than he possibly could."

Mrs. Balron laughed. "Of course you'd get more out of it, honey, so you might as well read it first. Come on, we'll go to my house where you can take your time in peace and quiet. That goonhead won't catch up with you for ages. My car's out in the driveway, but you'd better hide the book under your coat in case one of O.O.'s yokels notices it."

They went out the front door and circled around to where the yellow convertible was parked at the back.

"This book's heavy," Ada said as they climbed in. "Why didn't you use the front door? Everybody seems to come in the back way here."

"The front door was only for royalty and the old man. Hold on, now, I'm going to drive a little fast. I don't want them to catch us."

Ada kept her eyes closed for most of the trip. She managed to whisper once, "Slow down, will you? You'll have the whole town following us to find out what the disaster is."

"You leave this to me," Mrs. Balron said composedly. "I know what I'm doing."

She took Ada up to her own bedroom and established her on a chaise longue. "It's a useless bit of furniture, but it comes in handy for you now. I thought it was elegant when I bought it, but I've never had time to use it."

"How long have you had it?" Ada asked, settling back.

"Seven years. Actually, I have to buy a fancy robe to go with it, and I haven't got around to that yet. Now, make yourself comfortable and do your reading. You'll have plenty of time."

"Are you going to stay here?"

"No, no." Mrs. Balron picked up her purse and settled her hat. "I have to go back and stall them off. There's plenty of food in the icebox, so go down and get something to eat when you feel hungry."

Ada nodded, and Mrs. Balron went off and drove back to the big house. In the kitchen she came upon Annie and Pat talking together in low tones, and she stopped and gave them a suspicious eye.

Annie looked up at her. "Me and Pat been thinking about retiring a long time already, and I guess we'll do it right now. We'll maybe go to California."

"You'll maybe tie a noose around your necks," Mrs. Balron said coldly. "What do you suppose people will think if you skip now? I happen to know that you're both around my age, which is too soon for retiring. Do you want to sit around and watch moss growing in your elbows?"

"We don't know nothin' about all this trouble here," Annie declared indignantly.

Richard and the chief came into the kitchen, and the chief was scowling. "No book has legs to walk, so where is it? You and your wife had it. You ought to know where it is."

Mrs. Balron noticed that he had a blue leatherbound book under his arm and rightly assumed that it was Miss Violet's diary. She asked brightly, "What do you want with the book, anyway?"

The chief suppressed a very rude reply which sprang to his tongue, and Richard said, "I've already told you that someone came in during the night. I've no doubt he took it, whoever he was."

"I got to get my wife started on it right away," the chief said fretfully.

There was a sound of steps and voices from outside, and Judge Meeklyn, Doc Paunders, and Mr. Hernand came into the kitchen.

"We have only just heard about Miss Violet," Doc said gravely, "and of course we came at once. Is there anything we can do?"

The chief looked them over sourly. "You can find Miss Ivy's diary. Somebody walked off with it, and it's theft and I'll stick him inside for it."

The three men looked at each other, and then at the chief. Doc Paunders said, "There's some mistake, surely. We all know that neither of those girls ever kept a diary."

29

The chief thrust his jaw and Miss Violet's diary forward at the same time. "So you guys know all about it? Waddya call this? A collection of cooking receeps?"

Doc took the diary, and the three of them examined it. They admitted that it seemed to be Miss Violet's handwriting, but they maintained that both ladies had always scorned the idea of keeping a record of their activities.

"You gents got any idea what happened to Miss Ivy's diary?" the chief demanded.

"Certainly not," Judge Meeklyn said severely. "We have only just learned of the existence of this book, if it does exist."

"Well"—the chief turned his back on them—"seems I got to search the whole blamed house from attic to cellar."

This sounded like such a bore to Mrs. Balron that she spoke up. "Don't waste your time. It so happens that I know where the book is."

It took twelve minutes to get it out of her, and then the chief had to promise that he would not go at once and wrest it from Ada. Richard decided privately that the chief had no intention of keeping this promise, which was a correct assumption, but a phone call delayed him from flying out to his car. Everyone followed him to the library, and although he made furious gestures to disperse them, while he tried to listen at the same time, they huddled around him and strained their ears.

The chief cradled the phone at last and glared at his audience. "In case you'd all like to know, that was a call to advise me on the cause of death of Miss Violet Balron. And you got a fat chance learning any more about it, neither."

Judge Meeklyn straightened his shoulders. "Let us go, Doc. It seems that we can be of no assistance here."

The three of them departed, Mr. Hernand in Doc Paunders's car, and the judge driving away in his own.

"They're going to be lonely," Mrs. Balron observed. "It looks as though they won't even have Miss Dedingham."

"Have you seen her this morning?" Richard asked.

"No." Mrs. Balron pulled on her gloves. "I'm going home. There's nothing for me to do here. Annie, you get up off your tail and give this place a good cleaning, and Pat, you go on out to the garden. I want everything in perfect order when the madam returns."

Annie folded her arms over her stomach, and Pat set his various bones into stubborn immobility. Richard glanced at them and said, "The madam will not be returning, so take your time. And, Mother, you are to stay here or visit your friends, but you *are not to go home*. Is that clear?"

Mrs. Balron's jaw dropped for a moment before she brought it into vigorous use, but Richard interrupted her firmly. "If you go back home, I'll take the yellow convertible from you. It's in my name, and I can, and I *will*. Wait a minute, O.O. I'm coming with you."

He followed the chief outside, ignoring a variety of remarks flung after him by his mother, and caught up with him as he was getting into his car.

"Suppose I get the diary for you, O.O. I know you're busy."

"Nothing doing." The chief took out an enormous handkerchief and mopped his red face. "I got it figured, the same as you, that Miss Violet's 'dear friend' is gonna hot up his feet getting over there to get it. You think I want to see your smug map in the paper saying how you caught the murderer, and me shuffling my feet making a silly alibi?"

Richard shrugged. "You can't stop me from going over there, though."

"I want you to come over," the chief said, "and take your wife away and leave me get on with the job."

"What job? Do you suppose he isn't over there already? And do you actually think he won't disappear at once when he sees you go in, and me take my wife away without the diary?"

The chief banged the door of his car in a fury. "All right, go. But if you mess this up, I'll spread it all over town. You feel nice and sure it's one of those three old men, but me, I don't know a thing." He started the engine and bullied a protesting gear. "Just paste this in your hat. Miss Violet died of a heart attack."

Richard watched the car as it roared away, and then started towards the garage. Halfway, he turned abruptly and made for the yellow convertible. It might help to delay his mother a little, anyway.

Doc Paunders's car and Judge Meeklyn's were parked outside his mother's house, and he found the three men sitting in the living room with Ada, drinking coffee. He said, "Well! Pleasure to meet you all again so soon."

"We're very much upset about these diaries," Doc explained. "It's natural to suppose that we figure in them, and we feel there should be some assurance that the whole town won't be reading about us."

Richard nodded. "In a way, I agree with you. Have you finished Aunt Ivy's book yet, Ada?"

"No."

"Well, I'd suggest that you go and finish it now. If you decide there's nothing in it that would help the chief, we can do away with it. There's really no reason why the chief's wife should spread it far and wide."

Mr. Hernand sighed. "The chief already has Miss Violet's diary."

"Ada has read it." Richard sent her a meaning look. "There's absolutely nothing in it to embarrass you, is there, Ada?"

"No, nothing."

"That's understandable," Judge Meeklyn said heavily. "But Miss

Ivy was, er, more direct. I fear that her diary contains things which could hurt us all."

"You've nothing to worry about," Richard declared. "If you'll go now, Ada can finish it, but if you wait around, the chief will get here and take it away from her. If she decides we can't destroy the whole book, she can at least tear out any pages that are particularly damaging."

"I don't see why we can't destroy the whole book," Mr. Hernand said, and the other two nodded.

Richard shook his head. "The chief knows we have it."

Doc Paunders stretched his legs and grunted. "You run on and finish it, Miss Ada. We'll wait here."

Judge Meeklyn and Mr. Hernand agreed to this emphatically, and Ada left them and went upstairs. Richard paced the room in silence, wondering how he could get the three of them out of the house.

He gave up, in the end, and went upstairs. He found Ada in his mother's room on the chaise longue, and she gave him an inquiring look.

"Those three old pests are still sitting there, and I have to go. I want you to lock this door on the inside, and don't let any one of them in."

"Why?"

"You must realize that one of them killed Aunt Ivy. I believe he's insane. Will you lock the door?"

Ada shuddered and whispered, "Yes. Yes, I'll lock up."

"Good. Remember, you're not to let any one of them in, and if you need any help, wave something white at the front window. Somebody will be watching from across the street."

She nodded, and he went out and waited until he heard her lock the door. He descended and saw that the three men were talking in low tones, but he passed the living room, and went on out to the street. The chief was parked a short distance away, and he approached the car and leaned on the door. "I want you to put a man across the street from the house to watch for a possible distress signal."

"What for?"

Richard explained, and the chief first wanted to know who he thought he was, giving orders to the chief of police, and then sulkily dispatched a couple of men to watch the Balron home.

Richard drove into the town and unexpectedly came face to face with his mother. She had come in with the milkman, and she immediately took over the yellow convertible, and extracted from him a set of keys for the blue sedan. He let them go, but warned her again to stay away from the house.

"I haven't an idea in the world of going near the house," she told him airily. "It always reminds me of dishwashing and bed-making."

He went into the hotel to get lunch and immediately wished he hadn't. He was surrounded by people asking questions, and he was unable to get rid of them. He eventually pushed his way through to a table at the bar, and was surprised to find that Madge was sitting with him.

She said, "You know, Richard, that big old place is no good for you. It's too, well, elegant, and you really haven't the money for it."

"You're wrong about the money," Richard said mildly. "There's plenty. For elegance, of course, I must rely on Ada, but no doubt she'll be able to teach me. We intend to swing into full evening dress every night, and use the Royal china—"

He stopped suddenly, and stared over Madge's head. He'd forgotten all about the tea set. Was it still in the back seat of the yellow convertible, with his mother bouncing at high speed over every bump and stone in the countryside?

Madge hadn't noticed his abstraction and was talking steadily. "—naturally. Anyway, the will is like this—if Miss Violet died first, everything would go to you, but if Miss Ivy died first, which she did, Ada gets a quarter, and those three old men she considered her beaux get a quarter each."

30

Richard's eyes had been wandering around the room, but he jerked them back to stare at her. "What are you talking about?"

Madge gave him a hurt look.

"If you're talking about my aunts' wills, you're raving. They haven't been read yet."

"Not by you, perhaps. But their lawyer was relaxing here last night and asked me to have a drink with him."

"Get on with it, can't you?" Richard muttered.

"You mustn't be jealous, Richard. It was nothing. Anyway, it was a simple matter to get him to talk, although he warned me that it was all very confidential. It seems that the father had left his entire estate to his two daughters, but not in separate parts. The share of Miss Ivy, who was murdered, goes to Miss Violet, who was found dead this morning. Miss Ivy leaves you a pauper, but a lot goes to Ada. Now, I feel sure that you are not the sort of person who would live on his wife's money."

"You're so wrong," Richard said, grinning at her. "This changes the picture entirely. Now that my wife is rich she'll have to stay with me. I mean, she could hardly expect me to exist on the pittance I earn. Will you excuse me? I must go."

Madge seemed disinclined to excuse him, but he went, anyway, and took himself straight to the office of his aunts' lawyer. The gentleman was no longer relaxed and said several times that he really couldn't understand how such a thing could have happened. He also swore off liquor on the spot. It seemed, too, that Madge had got it wrong. Half of the estate was divided between Ada and Richard, and the other half divided among Miss Dedingham, Doc Paunders, Judge Meeklyn and Mr. Hernand. Originally, Miss Violet had left everything to Ada, but she had changed her will about six months ago.

Richard thanked him for the information and departed. He went to the chief's office and found him sitting at his desk, looking gloomy.

"Have you heard about this will business?" Richard demanded.

"Sure I've heard about it. You think I'm a dope?"

"Doesn't it help?"

"No. So one of those three old busters did it. You expect me to chain them together and lock-step them into the can? How do I know which one it is?"

"O.K.. If you sit there long enough, maybe the right one will walk in and hold out his hands for the cuffs."

Richard went out and decided to walk to the big house and get his car. He discovered that Annie was cleaning her own quarters and she declared that she was not going to stay in the big house alone because she was scared. He left her to it and got into his car.

He knew that he should go to the office for a while, but salved his conscience by deciding that he wouldn't be able to concentrate, any-way. He thought of the three old men, sitting and waiting. He ought to go back. He'd have to. One of them was a killer. And Miss Dedi-ngham had been there that night. Why? She must have been. She'd seen Miss Ivy move those chairs. Doc Paunders had assumed it was Miss Violet who'd moved them—remorse—and Judge Meeklyn and Mr. Hernand had concurred. Absurd. Miss Ivy had not been killed in the living room. There were no stains. It had happened in the cellar, and the stains wiped away afterward, the linoleum nailed to the board and put in place. And then Miss Violet came upstairs and changed the chairs in a fit of remorse? How could the three of them believe such a thing? He'd go and ask them. They didn't yet know about the other explanation in the diary. The right one, surely. It was like Miss Ivy. She'd figure that she had an equal chance of dying, and so it was quite honorable for them to fight it out so that the survivor might have everything her own way. And she'd started out by changing the chairs. Like her father, cold, no understanding, no sympathy. Miss Violet lying there watching her sister change the chairs, unable to get up and fight. And Miss Dedingham watching?

Richard shook his head. It was wrong, all wrong. Miss Violet watching the change of chairs, listening to the scream, and then able to run off to the big house and wander around. Of course not. She had died somewhere of a heart attack, and someone had carried her in. Why not leave her where she had died?

Her "dear friend" had certainly been in danger when he carried her into the house. Perhaps he had wanted to hide her for a while? No, he must have known she'd be found in that secret room. She'd picked the black iris and put them in the vase in the library, gone on up to the attic, taken pills, written in the diary, and *gone out after that*.

Richard sat up straight and shook his head. She wouldn't have done all that. She'd have run to someone and asked for help. Well, perhaps she'd run to Miss Dedingham and found her lying uncon-scious after the stroke. But what had Miss Dedingham been doing there, watching? Her business—that was it. Business of picking up antiques for sale. Only, why the little house? There were plenty of things in the big house. Well, of course the things he'd found in the little house had come from the big house.

Richard lighted a cigarette and rubbed his hand slowly across his forehead. These antique dealers often had clients who asked for specific things, and that was it. Miss Dedingham had a partner, one of those three old men. He'd borrow the electric from Miss Violet, certainly without Miss Ivy's knowledge, and Miss Dedingham would transact the business wearing her cameo pin and looking as much like Miss Ivy as possible. Certain things had been requested which were to be had only from the little house, so they picked them up and hid them in the cellar for a while, and if they were not missed, they carried them off. In this case, *he* had taken the things to the big house because he knew that they would shoot that night, and Miss Ivy would die. He'd put the bullets in Miss Violet's gun some time after Richard, himself, had been there. Had he asked Miss Dedingham to come over on business? To witness the fact that Miss Violet had done the actual shooting of her sister. Evidently he had intended to help Miss Violet to bury Miss Ivy in the cellar, probably figured that there would be less trouble if Miss Ivy simply disappeared. It might be generally assumed that she had gone off to live by herself. In any case, the thing misfired. The sisters had exchanged guns, and the bullet had missed Aunt Violet by a fraction. But she fell to the floor, and Miss Dedingham stood watching somewhere while Miss Ivy changed the chairs to the position she had always wanted. This must have been a bad shock for Miss Dedingham, and worse followed. The "dear friend" rushed in, berserk, picked up the hatchet, and fled after Miss Ivy to the cellar. Miss Dedingham's state of shock must have put her beyond any capability of helping Miss Violet. She'd managed to get herself home and had had a stroke. And Miss Violet? Had she got up and run out? No. She continued to lie there, because she was dead of a heart attack.

Richard took a long breath. It was taking shape now. Miss Dedingham hadn't gone straight home. She'd run, frightened and screaming, from the house, and through the rain to the big house, even beyond, but she'd come back and got in. She probably had a key. She went upstairs and wrote in the diary. Calmer by that time, she knew that she couldn't inform on the murderer without involving herself, but she could bring Miss Violet to life through her diary and at the same time do something that was extremely important to herself. Make it seem that Miss Violet had died *after* Miss Ivy, so that

Miss Ivy's will would stand, and Miss Dedingham would inherit money. The killer had tried to create that impression too, make it seem that Miss Violet had been wandering around in a daze. He picked the artificial black iris and put them in the big house because a lot of people knew that Miss Violet liked to pick flowers and knew that she sometimes picked the paper flowers along with the real.

So he'd had to gather up Miss Violet's slight body and take it home with him while he thought out what to do next, and when Miss Ivy was discovered he knew what he had to do. He picked the flowers and put them in an obvious place, and later, after the diaries had been taken from the little room, he took her up there. He knew about that room, but he didn't know about the diaries. They must have been a bit of a blow to him, but not too much. He didn't know about the final entry in Miss Violet's diary.

Richard sighed and started the car. He'd have to go to the chief and get him to put a handwriting expert on a sample of Miss Dedingham's writing.

The blue sedan ran out of gas directly opposite the little white house. Richard swore, and then decided to see whether the chief still had a man there, or if the chief were there himself.

There was no sign of O.O., but a man was lounging around at the back. He hailed Richard as a diversion from a dull assignment, and talked at some length about nothing very much. Richard ceased to listen when he realized that he was looking at a cellar entrance to the house.

31

Richard left the chief's man, who was saying wistfully that a beer would go good, and approached the cellar doors. He was certain that there was no outside door in that basement graveyard, so where did these lead to? And why had he never noticed them before? He reached down and pulled them open, to reveal steps that led down to an inner door.

"Hey!" The chief's man removed his body from the tree that had been supporting it. "You can't go in. Ain't nobody allowed in."

Richard had already gone down the steps, and he pulled open the inner door, which swung back easily. He found himself facing a blank stretch of unpainted plywood, and he pushed it tentatively. It was loose, but he had to pull it toward him, and he saw that it was hinged at one side. He stepped into the cellar and closed it after him, and it looked like a panel in the wall. It was banded in strips of wood like the other panels and was not in any way distinguishable from them.

He went out again and circled around the house to his car. He sighed at it, and then tramped off to the nearest gas station.

An attendant drove him back, and while the man was putting gas into the sedan Richard walked to the big house. Last night, he thought, or early in the morning, someone had brought Miss Violet in. The chief had assumed it was by the back door, since Ada had once found it unlocked, so he had searched carefully there at the back. Miss Violet had been dead too long to have walked in, so that he knew she had been carried. But Ada had heard someone go out the front door, and Miss Dedingham and her partner seemed to get in without trouble, so it seemed probable that they had a key. A key to the front door.

Richard went to the front and began to search around. He made his way slowly off the veranda to the narrow path that led to the driveway. It was of broken pavings with grass in the cracks, and the ground was soft after the rain, and presently he stopped, with a quick pull of his breath. There was a footprint between two of the pieces of pavement, clear, and already drying with sharply defined edges.

He called loudly for Pat, who eventually moved into sight wearing a look of badly strained patience.

"Look. This footprint. Did you make it?"

Pat gave it a contemptuous glance. "I did not. I got enough work around here without I make more for myself."

He raised his rake, and Richard made a frantic lunge for his arm. "You're not to touch it. Leave it exactly the way it is. And you're to stay here and see that no one else disturbs it. It's vitally important. I have to go and make a phone call."

Pat moved resignedly to an adjacent flower bed and muttered, "The two old wimmin was nuts, and it sure as hell runs in the family."

Richard went inside and tried to get the chief on the phone, but he was unable to get in touch with him. He went out again, and with a last warning to Pat to stay on guard, he hurried back to his car.

He drove to Mr. Hernand's house, where he knew the key was under the back-door mat, and picked up a shoe, and then went on to Judge Meeklyn's place. There was more difficulty here, and he had to climb through a cellar window in the end, but he got a shoe and made off with it and hoped that no one had seen him. Doc Paunders's shoe was a simple matter, since he always left his door open on the assumption that a stray patient might wander in. It was lucky, Richard thought, that the three of them had been out of his way, waiting for Ada to finish the diary.

He hurried back to the big house, and found Pat still guarding the footprint but showing signs of incipient revolution.

"You think I got all day to stand here waitin' for you? And then you'll be yappin' how I don't get my work done."

"Your work is to follow the instructions of your new employer."

"My *noo* employer? Who inherited me to you, anyways?"

Richard was on his knees in the grass with Doc Paunders's shoe carefully suspended over the print, but it did not seem to fit. He tried the other two, and had no better luck, and Pat asked severely, "Where did you get them shoes?"

The chief's car came blazing up the driveway and stopped with a hysterical protest by the brakes. The chief struggled out from behind the wheel and came lunging over to them.

"What is it? What have you got there?"

Richard showed him the footprint.

The chief turned to Pat. "You make that print?"

"I ain't gonna stand for it!" Pat said furiously. "People steppin' all over my grass and the stoopid police askin' me did I do it myself! I'm gonna get on with the work I'm paid for, and I'm gonna sue to get my taxes back on the salary you ain't earnin'." He turned his outraged back and marched off, and the chief mopped his hot face.

"What are you carrying all those there shoes around for?" he demanded peevishly.

Richard explained and added, "They don't seem to fit the print."

"What about your foot?"

"Mine?"

"Sure. You think you got diplomatic immunity, or something?"

Richard balanced on his left leg and suspended his right foot above the print. It was obviously too big.

"O.K., O.K.. You don't have to stand there like a damn stork."

Richard regained his balance and said, "Of course, these are not the shoes they wore today."

"Yeah, maybe that's it. We got to get the ones on them now. I'll have someone herd the old busters out here."

"Fine. And when you get a fit what are you going to do? Accuse him of murder because he stopped to sniff a bloom and got one foot on the grass?"

"Nuts."

"I want you to get a handwriting expert. And did you ever find the little hatchet?"

"Sure we found it. It was lying outside in the rain and mud, and there was nothing on it but rain and mud, neither."

"Do you know about the cellar entrance in the little house?"

"I not only know about, I know who did the work on that cellar. Mr. Hernand took care of it. He sublet the contract to Doc Paunders, and Judge Meeklyn got Miss Dedingham's handyman to do the job with the aid of a boy. What do you want with a handwriting expert?"

Richard scratched his ear and murmured, "I'll tell you. But what was all that about the work in the cellar?"

"Why don't you listen? Mr. Hernand got the contract from your aunts, and made the most money, because he gave a bit less to Doc to get it done, and Doc asked the judge to recommend a guy to do it. They all made something out of it, including Miss Dedingham."

"It sounds as though my aunts had been surrounded with vultures."

"Don't talk so foolish. The old dames had plenty of money, so why should they be bothered with details?"

Richard shrugged. "About the shoes. I think your best bet would be to get the ones they're wearing today, after they go to bed tonight."

"What do you think I am?" the chief demanded indignantly. "Telling me to sneak into people's homes and steal their shoes! By rights, I ought to pinch you for stealing the ones you got there."

"Nothing doing. These are mine, and I was figuring on taking them to the shoemaker."

The yellow convertible leaped up the driveway and stopped directly behind the chief's car with no more than an inch between them. Mrs. Balron climbed out and approached, talking volubly.

"What the devil do you think you're doing, blocking up the driveway like that? Don't you know that you ought to set an example in good driving? What would you say if I slapped my car in the driveway down at police headquarters?"

"Try it and see," the chief said coldly. "I got enough on you now to revoke your license."

"Mother will contribute twenty-five dollars to the Police Benefit," Richard said, "and serve her right."

"What are you doing with those shoes?" Mrs. Balron asked.

Richard swung them idly. "I was pretending that they belong to Mr. Hernand, Doc Paunders, and Judge Meeklyn, and trying to fit them into that footprint, there."

"You're drooling, son."

"No. The chief would have to arrest me for stealing if I admitted that the shoes were not mine."

"Oh," Mrs. Balron nodded.

The chief spat into the flower bed, and Mrs. Balron closed her eyes tightly and shuddered.

Richard said, "I'm convinced that Aunt Violet didn't write that last entry in her diary. We must look into that angle. This shoe business is a flop. None of them fits."

"If we could only try the shoes they got on now," the chief muttered.

Mrs. Balron neatly dispatched a wasp from her sleeve. "That's not at all necessary."

"You sure know a lot," the chief said sourly. "It might be you could tell me which one of those guys murdered Miss Ivy."

"No 'might be' about it. I could." She rooted around in her purse until she found a measuring tape, and then she kneeled down and carefully measured the footprint. Still kneeling on the grass, she measured the three shoes, and at last held one up.

"The man who owns this shoe, and I know the owner, is, I presume, the man who murdered Miss Ivy."

32

Richard and the chief stared at the shoe, and Mrs. Balron got up and dusted off her skirt.

She went off to the front door, where she rang the bell and waited.

The chief scratched his head. "I'll have to talk to him. You coming?"

Richard nodded, and they walked slowly toward the chief's car. Mrs. Balron left the front door and called to them. "Where's Annie?"

Richard looked around. "She's not there. Who are you visiting, anyway? You know that neither the master nor the mistress is at home."

"I know that I've been forbidden the use of my own home, and I supposed that I'd be welcome here to rest my aching feet. Where are you two going?"

"We're going to talk to him."

"You can't do it that way." She might have been talking to a pair of children. "You'll put him on his guard, and there isn't enough evidence. You have to trap him."

"Sure," said the chief, "trap him. Maybe you know how to do that. We're only a couple of dumb males."

Mrs. Balron tapped her teeth with a fingernail. "Where is he now?"

"Never mind."

"Oh, I know. They're all at my house. You follow me, and let me do the talking."

"No!" the chief cried in a stricken voice.

Mrs. Balron was already on her way to the yellow convertible.

"Come on," the chief said desperately. "We got to get there before she does."

He ran his car around the circular drive in front of the house, with the yellow convertible on his tail, honking at intervals. He said to Richard from the corner of his mouth, "Don't do her any good to sit on her horn. We're ahead of her and we'll get there first."

He should have known her better. Mrs. Balron, irked to the limit of her endurance, cut across the lawn, circled around him, and swept onto the road and out of sight.

"That settles it," the chief said with deadly calm. "When I catch up with her I'm gonna put her under arrest."

"What's the charge?" Richard asked. "She ruined some grass, but it's on private property."

"I'll slap it on her for speeding."

"How are you going to prove it? I didn't see her."

When they arrived the yellow convertible was parked at the curb, and inside, Ada and Mrs. Balron sat in the living room, but there was no sign of the three men.

Ada stood up. "O.O., I read the diary, and there is nothing in it to bother those three men. They went home. Mrs. Balron is driving me to the big house to get my things. I shall have to get back to New York. I've rehearsals coming up."

Mrs. Balron nodded. "Perhaps you'd like to go with Ada, son?"

The chief put a cold sneer on his face. "I thought you had some business to attend to?"

"Oh." Mrs. Balron nodded again. "I'll do it on my way over. You go back to your office. He'll be along shortly."

"You don't say?"

"I do say."

"You want to bet?"

Mrs. Balron turned back from the doorway. "Ten dollars?"

"Twenty." The chief stroked his chin. "Let's make it twenty."

"Good. I didn't think it was right to take that much from you, but since you ask for it it's settled."

She pushed Ada outside and shut the door firmly behind her.

The chief looked helplessly at Richard. "I'm going out to his house."

"If you don't go to your office for a while, you'll forfeit the twenty because you won't be able to prove that he didn't come."

The chief stalked out, muttering rude words, and Richard followed him. "Drop me somewhere, will you? I want to get to my wife before she makes off."

"O.K.. Wait until I go across the street and send those poor dopes home. They're still waiting for a distress signal from the window, on your fool instructions."

"I think they're asleep," Richard said. "Wake them up and threaten them with a switch to the street-cleaning department."

Richard was dropped at a convenient corner, and he went on to the big house. His mother was wandering around at the front, but he avoided her and went to the back, through the kitchen, and upstairs.

Ada was in her bedroom, attempting to close a suitcase, and he went in quietly and asked, "May I help you?"

She jumped, and turned a startled face.

"Sorry, it's these heavy carpets. It's quite a house, isn't it? Unfortunate that it will have to be sold. Cheap, too. No one in town could afford to keep it up, except the two of us, together."

Ada said, "I'll push down this side while you push down the other side."

Richard put his hand on the suitcase, but instead of pushing down he flung the lid open. "What's the matter with you? You can't leave before the funerals."

Ada pulled the lid down again. "I *have* to leave before the funerals. I need the part, and I'll lose it if I wait. I'm sorry about the fool marriage, but it's as much your fault as mine."

Richard opened the lid. "You won't go to your aunts' funerals simply because you're peeved with me and want to show me. So you won't pay that last respect to two old ladies who were very good to you."

"All right, I'll stay, but I'll stay at the hotel."

"You know what they would have thought of that."

"Oh, don't be so absurd!" Ada pushed the hair from her hot face and glared at him.

"I'm merely trying to get you to stay here with me."

"Will you *please*," said Ada, "help me to shut this suitcase?"

Richard helped her, and they had just snapped the locks when Mrs. Balron walked into the room. "What on earth's been keeping you, Red?"

"You go along," Richard told her. "I'll bring Ada. It'll take her a few minutes."

Mrs. Balron eyed the closed suitcase and Ada, who was dressed even to her suit and hat, while her gloves and bag lay on the bed. "I see. Well, I hate to act like a mother-in-law, but let me give you a piece of advice, Ada. Get out while the getting is good. You have a promising part, and I believe you can rise to the heights. Stay here, and you'll be a measly housewife."

"In this house I'll be a measly housewife? I'll have a maid and a gardener, and allover carpeting. First lady of the countryside."

"Talk sense," Mrs. Balron said practically. "One maid can't take care of this museum."

"I could do some housework in the early morning, while no one was looking."

Richard nodded. "And I can do something on the nights we don't have brilliant company. We intend to dress for dinner every night, and you can't call anyone who does that a measly housewife."

"You seem to have made up your minds." Mrs. Balron shook her head. "*You'll* find out, but it's not on my conscience because I've warned you."

She was off before Ada could stop her, and Richard opened the suitcase again.

The chief was sitting in his office, looking at his folded hands, when Doc Paunders walked in.

"I want to confess to the murder of Miss Ivy," Doc said cheerfully.

33

The chief had to swallow twice before he was able to say, "Sit down. I'll get a stenographer."

"I fell in love with Miss Ivy in our very young days," Doc Paunders said thoughtfully, "and maybe that's why I hated her so much later on. Anyway, she wanted to marry me against her father's wishes, but I wouldn't do it, couldn't let her lose all that money just for me. I didn't want to lose the money, either. I thought I'd hang around for a few years and win the old man over, but Ivy wouldn't even introduce me to him. Said she couldn't. We broke up over that.

"After a while I began seeing Miss Violet at the tea room in town, and I fell in love with her. She was much sweeter and more amiable, and she introduced me to her father, too, but all he said was, 'Excuse me, but I don't care to know you.' Typical of him. Anyway, Violet agreed to wait until he could be brought around. Hernand was in the picture, too. After her fortune—he loves money.

"Well, Ivy never forgave me for switching my affections to Violet. The years passed and the old man wouldn't give in, and I wasn't mean enough to marry either one of them without the money, because they were used to high living and no work. We drifted apart, but after the old man died I thought Violet and I could get married. Only, would you believe it? Ivy stood in our way. She kicked up a ruckus, said I was after Violet's mone. Iit wouldn't be fair for Violet to leave her. I got Violet to promise to marry me, anyway, and then I discovered that if she did, her entire estate would revert to Ivy. I could hardly believe it. The old devil still trying to control their actions from his grave. Hernand was still hanging around, and I thought if we both married them at the same time, the money would be safe. But no. Ivy laughed in our faces. *She* wasn't ever going to get married.

"Those two girls took to fighting all the time, about marriage, and who they'd leave the money to. One night, I took a walk up that way, and saw them shooting at each other. It jolted me pretty badly, and I talked to Violet and put blanks in their guns.

"Judge Meeklyn had moved in on us, and he made up his mind he'd like to marry Violet, too. Miss Dedingham was mad as a hornet because she thought he wanted her. But he didn't, he wanted the money. Miss Dedingham knew about the shooting games. She'd seen them while she was walking, and asked them about it. They told her, and also told her to mind her own business, which she did.

"I got more and more in debt, and I got so desperate that I crept around and put a bullet in Violet's gun. It was there for weeks, and Ivy never got it, so I went around to put in more, and they walked in on me. I had the gun in my hand, and I didn't hear them until they opened the front door. I had no time to think of anything. I just flopped down flat on my face, wondering what I'd say to them. It worked out all right because they took one look at me and ran off yelling. I had enough time to get home before Richard and the sisters arrived. I went in later that night, to the cellar to get some things, but Richard started coming down, and I had to fade.

"Then there was that wedding, those two trying to get the money for themselves. I was feeling pretty depressed about it, and then I heard the girls fighting in an undertone about the chairs. They were getting pretty worked up, and I figured they might decide to shoot it out.

"I returned later to watch them from the hall. It was easy for me to move around their house without being seen. They were upstairs getting ready when I arrived. They liked to be neat in case the undertaker had to be called in, and I filled Violet's gun with bullets. It was puzzling, too, when I opened it. There wasn't even the one I'd put there before.

"They came downstairs, and just as they aimed, Ivy said, 'Let's hope we can shoot better this way.' I didn't know what she meant until they pulled the triggers and Violet fell. Then I knew. They'd decided to exchange guns. Ivy immediately changed the chairs, and I rushed her. I picked up that little hatchet and swung. She ran off through the dining room to the kitchen, and then it was that I saw Miss Dedingham was with us. The cellar door was open a little, since that was the way she'd come in, and Ivy ran down there. She was trapped. She didn't know about that panel door leading outside, so I got her. I finished her off and buried her in the grave I'd made for her some time ago. You see, I figured when Violet *did* get her you'd never believe the story they'd planned, that the one who was dead had shot herself accidentally, because the shot would have come from too far away, and it seemed probable that no one would ever find Ivy's body in that grave in the cellar. In that case, Violet would eventually get all the money. I'd wrapped up some things for Miss Dedingham to sell, and hidden them in the grave, but I took them out to make room for the body."

"How long have you and Miss Dedingham been selling things from the Balron estate?" the chief asked.

"Oh"—Doc stretched his legs and patted his stomach—"for a while."

"How did you get in and out of the big house?"

"I have a key for the front door, took it off Violet's key ring. Anyway, where was I? Oh yes. I came up from the cellar when I had finished with Ivy and discovered that Violet was dead, although she had not been shot, and Miss Dedingham had disappeared. I was pretty scared, but I tried to think it out, and I decided that she'd gone straight home. I didn't believe she'd go to the big house because of the honeymoon couple being there. First, though, I had to get Violet out, and the bloodstains washed away. I did that quickly, and then carried Violet to my car and drove to my house. I carried her in and put her in the office and locked the door. I drove back and ran over to Miss Dedingham's and banged on the door, but there was no answer. It was open, as usual, so I went in, and found her lying on the floor. She'd had a stroke, but she was conscious and moaning. I got her onto her bed and told her I'd be back with something to relieve her pain.

"I began to think it might be a good alibi for me. I couldn't know she'd already been to the Balron big house and written a complete description of everything she'd seen.

"I returned to my car and went back home. I changed my clothes, got rid of mud and blood on the suit and shoes. It was late by that time, and that was my downfall, of course. It was too late. I drove to Hernand's and picked him up, told him that Miss Dedingham had telephoned for help. When we got there she was in a coma.

"Well, after Richard had been in Hernand and I started looking through the house for Violet, and I had to put on a good act. Mrs. Balron turned up, and Hernand and I went off. I'd left Violet on a chair, and rigor was already established, and I didn't know what to do.

"Everyone seemed to think that Violet was still living, which was what I wanted, and I thought I'd further the idea a little. I saw those black iris Pat had put in, so I picked them and put them in the house in a vase.

"But I had to get her out of my house, and I decided to put her in the attic room, the one they retired to every now and then. I knew she'd be found there. She was light, and I carried her out the side door and put her into my car, late in the night, of course. They used to keep the keys to that room around their necks, and I was annoyed to find Violet didn't have hers on. I thought I'd have to put her in another room.

"I nearly got caught in the big house. Lights kept going on and off. When things seemed to be quiet, I took Violet up. It made me puff a bit, but when I got up I found that room open, and I saw it for the first time. I didn't think about the key then, but I know now that Miss Dedingham must have had one. They used to allow her in there. She must have known about the diaries. Mrs. Balron told me she wrote about me in Violet's book, and after all I'd done for her, too.

"When I came down there were lights on in the library, but I slipped out the front door and hid behind a clump of bushes and waited, and finally I got back to my car. I felt pretty good, matter of fact. I'd covered up cleverly. A perfect job, and marred by one wretched bit of bad luck. An idle woman's curiosity."

34

The chief was sitting alone in his office, drumming his fingers on the desk, when Mrs. Balron and Madge walked in.

"Hey!" Mrs. Balron hailed him. "This town really ought to be jacked up. Madge just missed the last train to New York, and there isn't another until tomorrow morning."

"So you want me to wipe away a tear? Tomorrow morning will roll around."

"Mother might change her mind by tomorrow," Madge said. "Surely you can have a train flagged, or something."

"What you think we got a stationmaster for?"

"I've often wondered," Mrs. Balron said impatiently. "We asked him, and he just let his mouth drop open."

The chief shrugged. "He's not so dumb. He answered you, and saved his breath at the same time."

"Very well," Madge said resignedly, "then I shall wait until to-morrow." She turned and started out of the office.

"Don't you want me to drive you home?" Mrs. Balron called after her.

"No, no. No, indeed, the walk will do me good." Madge disappeared from sight in a hurry.

"People as a whole," said Mrs. Balron, "are entirely too touchy."

The chief leaned back in his chair. "While you're here—how did you find out that Miss Dedingham had written that last piece in the diary? *I* didn't know. I was gonna send for a handwriting guy."

Mrs. Balron sniffed. "You waste so much time trying to be clever. Richard said he didn't think Miss Violet had written it, so I figured that the only other one who even knew about the diaries was Miss Dedingham. *They'd* never tell their boy friends they were keeping diaries. I was sure Miss Dedingham must have seen *something* that night, so I told Doc she'd written it all out. I said, the chief has it, and if you run away you'll probably be caught, and if you're not caught, you won't have any money to live on. If you give yourself up, they'll go easy on you. I pointed out to him that the jail is very comfortable since the Ladies' Rain or Shine Club fixed it up, and he'd be right here in town—"

The chief wiped his face with the palm of his hand and muttered, "I think I'll resign."

"Oh, you needn't do that." Mrs. Balron headed for the door. "Just call on me when you need help."

* * *

Richard, driving the blue sedan, was saying, "Don't tell me I really wanted to marry Madge. *I* should know how I feel."

"I'll tell you and you'll listen," Ada declared. "I want to get things straight. You see, I got my new part only because the old fool who stars in the thing took a shine to me. I tried to keep away from him, but somehow he was always there, so when you suggested an engagement of course I welcomed it. I thought it would shut up the wife, who was getting nasty. Just why I went through with the marriage, I wouldn't know. I'm sorry, and I'll pull out as soon as possible so that you and Madge—"

Richard swung to the side of the road and stopped the car. "Stop trying to stuff Madge down my throat, will you? Can't you and I quit being secretly in love, and bring it out into the open?"

Ada picked at her skirt with agitated fingers and muttered, "I should have my head examined for giving up my theatrical career, like this."

THE END

If you enjoyed this book by Constance & Gwenyth Little ask your bookseller for the other nineteen titles by these sisters reprinted by The Rue Morgue Press. The twenty-first and final title is scheduled to be reprinted later in 2007. For information on The Rue Morgue Press turn the page.

About the Rue Morgue Press

"Rue Morgue Press is the old-mystery lover's best friend, reprinting high quality books from the 1930s and '40s."
—*Ellery Queen's Mystery Magazine*

Since 1997, the Rue Morgue Press has reprinted scores of traditional mysteries, the kind of books that were the hallmark of the Golden Age of detective fiction. Authors reprinted or to be reprinted by the Rue Morgue include Catherine Aird, Dorothy Bowers, Pamela Branch, Joanna Cannan, Glyn Carr, Torrey Chanslor, Clyde B. Clason, Joan Coggin, Manning Coles, Lucy Cores, Frances Crane, Norbert Davis, Elizabeth Dean, Constance & Gwenyth Little, Marlys Millhiser, James Norman, Stuart Palmer, Craig Rice, Kelley Roos, Charlotte Murray Russell, Maureen Sarsfield, Margaret Scherf and Juanita Sheridan.

To suggest titles or to receive a catalog of Rue Morgue Press books write P.O. Box 4119, Boulder, CO 80306, telephone 800-699-6214, or check out our website, www.ruemorguepress.com, which lists complete descriptions of all of our titles, along with lengthy biographies of our writer